"I won't let you make a fool of me."

Elvi's voice was breathless. "I—I won't be seduced by you!"

"Seduced?" Rodari laughed. "I am asking you to marry me! I am not suggesting that you spend the night with me in a mountain hut."

"You...you don't seem to be a marrying man." The desperation of love and panic grew acute, and all at once Elvi found herself fighting to evade his touch. "You haven't mentioned love!" The words broke from her. "Love and marriage are supposed to go together."

"Like tea and toast," he mocked.

"There...you make a jest of it and expect me to take your proposal seriously," Elvi retorted. "Let's go back to the hotel and forget that for one mad moment you fancied to marry me!"

VIOLET WINSPEAR
is also the author of these books in

Harlequin Presents Collection

Many of these titles are available at your local bookseller.

VIOLET WINSPEAR

bride of lucifer

Originally published as Harlequin Presents #30

Harlequin Books

TORONTO • LONDON • LOS ANGELES • AMSTERDAM
SYDNEY • HAMBURG • PARIS • STOCKHOLM • ATHENS • TOKYO

Harlequin Presents edition published December 1973
ISBN 0-373-15019-9

Second printing July 1974
Third printing August 1974
Fourth printing May 1976
Fifth printing September 1976
Sixth printing February 1977
Seventh printing March 1977
Eighth printing December 1978

This *Harlequin Presents Collection* edition published June 1981

Original hardcover edition published in 1971
by Mills & Boon Limited

CHAPTER I

FROM the moment he had given her the ring she had felt both thrilled and a tiny bit fearful. The stone was a finely carved ruby of exquisite colour, in a setting of small perfect diamonds. He had said quite casually that the ring was a heirloom and had been in his family for many generations. It had a Latin look, as Rodari had himself. A distinguished and dashing look that spoke of breeding and the privileges of wealth.

Could it be real that he wanted and needed her? What had she to offer a man who could have taken for his bride a girl of beauty and wealth, poise and wit?

The high-powered car sped along a road that offered glimpses of vineyards and bean terraces, and the black furrows ploughed by white oxen. The sun was shining through a cloud, and when Elvi glanced at the man who had made her his with a ring and a vow in a Roman church she felt again that cold rush of panic, that crazy urge to escape before it was too late. Yet even as she sat there beside him, stricken by panic, she knew that if he stopped the car and threw open the door for her she would not find the nerve or the will to flee from him.

Rodari Fortunato, driving her to his villa on the Isola Fortunato and saying not a word to her on this their wedding day.

Could he be regretful already? Did she see it stamped

5

on his profile, a deep-etched line of tension, knotting in his jaw, beating visibly beneath the skin that was deeply tanned after a winter in the Italian Alps, where he had skiied almost all the time and where it had been whispered among the other guests at the hotel that he was recovering from a great unhappiness.

Elvi had been working at the hotel as a nurse, for nursing was her profession and skiers often came to grief and had to be looked after, and the Alpine surroundings of the hotel had made the work pleasant for the young English girl.

"Will it be dark by the time we reach the island?" she asked. Though Rodari lived mainly in Rome, where he had a suite of rooms, he had thought she might enjoy a honeymoon at his ancestral home. She was innocently unaware that her question held her fear of him as well as her feeling of love. She wanted to belong to him, but they had known each other so short a time, and everything had happened so swiftly, that she felt as if she had been pursued and needed to catch her breath.

The road ahead of them was a patchwork of sun and shadow, and the occasional traffic consisted of farm carts and one or two old-fashioned motors. Rodari glanced at her and lifted a dark eyebrow in a teasing way.

"Yes, it will be dark, but there will be lights on the boat that will take us across to the villa. Though I return home so rarely these days there is a housekeeper and her husband to run the place for me. My parents are dead, as I told you. My grandmother and my sister Elena live together just outside Rome, so I see them quite often. Do you now feel more reassured? A meal will be awaiting us. The villa will be warm and clean, and our beds will be aired." He gave a rather sardonic laugh. "You English people seem to worry over trifles, yet you remain so calm in a crisis."

"We are of a different temperament from Latins," she
6

admitted. "But I'm not worrying all that much over the domestic arrangements at the villa. I'm sure everything will be fine ... I couldn't imagine a man like yourself accepting anything but the best."

An acute little silence followed her words and she bit her lip. Was he thinking that she was not as lovely or as poised as the girl he might have married? Everyone at the hotel had hinted that he grieved over a broken romance.

They motored past a small valley frothing with almond blossom, and her fingers stole over the ruby that felt so strange on her slender hand. White and pink blossom for a wedding. Diamonds for desire ... sudden tears in her eyes that she had to blink away. Was it on the rebound that Rodari had married her today in that Roman church with lilies and candles on the altar?

"You have gone suddenly quiet," he said.

"So have you."

"Ah, are we about to have our first tiff?"

"Of course we aren't. I was admiring those almond trees in blossom." She brushed her flyaway hair from her eyes; long brown-gold hair released from its neat chignon and a contrast to her clear grey eyes. Beneath her cheekbones lay small pools of shadow, and her mouth was all compassion.

"You need to eat," said Rodari. "I have heard that girls don't eat very much on their wedding day."

A little later he stopped at a farmhouse and they had lunch, followed by Tuscan figs and coffee. They took with them a pink melon which they ate later by the roadside, with a soft purple dusk falling down over the Tuscan fields. The fruit was sweet as honey, and the rich black earth smelled of the crops growing in regular rows. This was the land of Rodari's birth ... Elvi was a young nurse who had come to Italy on impulse, having no one to please but herself.

"Have you ever tasted fruit as good as that before?" A

7

smile gleamed in his dark eyes as he leaned forward and let his hand rest against her wind-cooled cheekbone. "We have a few miles more to go, so why don't you take a nap while I drive?"

"All right." She felt the lingering warmth of his touch as she slid down in her seat and pulled the soft fur collar of her coat about her face. She had never possessed a fur coat before, and this one was so smooth and glossy that it must have cost a great deal of money. He had swung it about her shoulders in a casual manner, just as he had slid on to her finger the ruby ring.

His to dress and adorn . . . but did he truly love her?

Rodari Fortunato, whose novels about Rome had in the last few years been made into a series of fine films, acclaimed by the public and the critics alike as deep and rich and real; stories that touched the heart and the conscience.

He was famous and attractive, yet something had driven him to the Alps in search of forgetfulness, and there he had befriended Elvi, had taken her out and taught her to ski. And there with the moon shining over the peaks, a silver night that clung to her senses like the strands of a web, he asked her to be his wife. It could only be a little moon madness on his part, she told herself, and with a little laugh she turned to gaze at the Alps and she said lightly: "You shouldn't go around saying such things, *signore*. One of these nights a lonely girl might take you at your word and expect you to marry her."

"Are you lonely, Elvi?" The hard warmth of his hands closed on her shoulders and he made her look at him. "I have often wondered if you might be, the shy stranger among a lot of sophisticated tourists, going about your work with such a dedicated air. Some of them must make trying patients."

"I enjoy my profession, *signore*," she replied. "And it makes an interesting change to work abroad."

"Would you like to live in Italy?" His hands tightened on her shoulders until he seemed to want to hurt her. "With me?"

"Please . . . you mustn't talk about marrying me." All at once the panic of finding herself in response to his touch had swept over her. It would be all too easy in the moonlight to believe that he meant what he said, but when morning came she would have to face the bleak reality of waking from a dream. She was only a nurse, with a face more quiet than pretty, and with resolution she fought the weakness, and the longing, which she felt at his nearness.

"You would be bored with me within a few days," she said breathlessly. "The Chianti we had with our dinner has gone to your head, and to mine, but I won't let you make a fool of me. I – I won't be seduced by you!"

"Seduced?" He laughed and the wind blew his black hair. "I am asking you to marry me! I am not suggesting that you spend the night with me in a mountain hut."

"You . . . you don't seem to me a marrying man." The desperation of love and panic grew acute and all at once she found herself fighting to evade his touch. But it was like trying to escape the tide when it rushes in. Like a moth battering its fragile wings against a tree. He was so much taller than Elvi; so devastating in his charming arrogance and his determination to have his own way.

"You haven't mentioned love!" The words broke from her. "Love and marriage are supposed to go together."

"Like tea and toast?" he mocked.

"There . . . you make a jest of it and expect me to take your proposal seriously."

"Don't let us be too serious, my girl of the English woods." He pushed a hand through her windblown hair and then gripped the softness of it as if something drove him to be a little cruel . . . the memory, perhaps, of hair more raven, or of a girl less reserved and more willing to

9

respond to his Latin impetuosity.

"Love?" he murmured. "Have you ever considered what it is, Elvi? A condition of the heart that makes the pulse race and the mind confused. It's like a fever, and the remedy for it is a cool hand on the forehead and some gentle care."

"You sound as if you need a nurse instead of a wife, Rodari." Her own pulse was racing as she spoke; her own mind was confused. She wanted to give in to him, to let his strange need of her sweep over her . . . yet where in the end would it land her? A marriage based on a man's need for some peace and quiet was a poor substitute for a marriage of love. She had known him two weeks and she knew that he found her company pleasing, he had a fondness for her, but what would happen when he, a man of the world, grew bored with his quiet bride?

"Let us go back to the hotel," she pleaded. "Let us forget that for a mad moment you fancied to marry me."

"Are you trying to make me believe that you don't care for me?" His eyes held a rather wicked smile as he gazed down at her, holding her so she felt the promise of pain if she tried to escape him. They had a snowy plateau to themselves, and they stood there like dark etchings in the moonlight, figures in a dream set against a tapestry of icy peaks and pine-trees, the roof of a mountain chalet just visible through the cluster of trees.

Suddenly it angered her that he should be so sure of her. "I have my career, *signore*. I wouldn't give that up for the dubious honour of being married for my cool touch and my ability to make myself scarce when not needed."

"Don't forget the little flashes of temper," he laughed. "No Italian would want a woman lacking in spirit. Come, you will have all the career you need in being with a man whose own career is so hectic. Elvi, I propose to you tonight because tomorrow I return to Rome. If you

10

wish to become my wife then you must decide right now, or say goodbye to me in the morning."

At these words she felt a physical sinking of the heart. Everything seemed to go from silver to grey, and the very air turned icy cold. She didn't want to say goodbye to him, but the alternative was a marriage she dare not risk. To love and not be loved in return was to invite unhappiness at some future date.

"I shan't forget you, Rodari." Her voice shook, her whole being trembled as he enclosed her face with his hands and made her look at him in the light of the Alpine moon.

"I shall not forget you," he said. "You brought into my life the quality of mercy, most refreshing to a man in my profession. I hoped to hold you, but if you insist that I let you go . . . do you insist, Elvi? Is it me you're afraid of, or my friends and associates who may feel that a man should marry to suit his public life rather than his private one?"

"You are an important man . . . you're a member of Roman society and you travel all over the world. You need a wife who can cope with the demands of your life. I could only make a fiasco of being the wife of a famous writer whose books are filmed. You told me you write the film scripts and mix with the people who act in films. The very thought of them terrifies me."

"I can feel you trembling," he drawled. "My dear child, what is there to be terrified of in sharing my life and my friends? You won't be alone as you are now to fend for yourself in a world of demanding strangers. Come, I want you to share my life."

"Because I shall never make demands on you?" she asked quietly.

"Because you are candid and honest, Elvi. You have no pretensions and no secrets. You are real and not an actress."

"An actress?" she echoed, and her heart quickened. "You must know quite a few of them."

"Of course."

"Did you ever care for one of them?" It was as if the question came of its own accord, from the lips of a puppet. It was a petty, foolish, naïve thing to ask, and she had to close her eyes against the faintly scornful smile with which he received it.

"I am thirty-four and hardly a cloistered monk. Did you hope to marry a man who had never touched another woman? You might be innocent enough to hope for that, and young enough to believe that such a rarity would make a good husband. I fear you would be in for a disappointment."

"Y-you are talking about lovemaking." Her cheeks burned. "I'm talking about love."

"Do you love me, child?" He stroked her hair and this time his hand was gentle. "Are you afraid I shall not make you happy? I admit to possessing temper and pride . . . but I can be kind."

"No . . . don't get around me with kindness!" Even as she resisted him there was a sudden roar from above and a small avalanche of snow broke loose from the heights and came tumbling down. She was swept to one side in his arms and the next instant they had fallen together into a snowdrift, and pillowed there she felt his kiss as the snow from above rushed past and the moon shot the scene with silver and shadow.

"Don't . . . please!"

But her pleading was as nothing, melting and dying like flakes of snow beneath the warmth of his mouth. "Rodari . . . why me?"

"Because you have nobody . . . but me."

Possessive, almost frightening words, so that like a bird she was thrilled to stillness there in his arms, with his face above hers, etched clear in every detail by the moon-

12

light. His features were lean, shaven, with deep lines impressed in the Italian darkness of his skin. His eyes at the moment were dark, but in the daylight she had seen cornelian flashes in them. The smooth hair at his temples was silver-flecked. At their first meeting the distinction of the man had overawed her. She had wondered if he ever smiled, for in those first few days there seemed to be a sardonic twist to his lips. Then he had begun to notice her in her white uniform and the shadow of a smile seemed to move about in his eyes ... as if he found her amusing. He had stood in the foyer one day and barred her way as she was going out for a walk. She saw the white line of his teeth bite upon his dark cigar, and something gripped her heart. She had known in that moment that he could be remorseless, yet when he asked if he could walk with her she had not denied him.

She had not dreamed that their walk together would lead to a proposal of marriage on a mountainside.

"Say yes," he murmured, close against her ear. "Say it now and don't think about it."

The snow was falling about them like cool torn petals, settling on the thick darkness of his hair silvered at the temples, tiny metal wings, glinting like his eyes. She wanted to say no, but the snow was numbing her lips. She knew her face was ghostly, there against the darkness of his sleeve. She noticed the hollows under his cheekbones, as if he hungered for a love he had lost and sought some consolation with a girl who could never hurt him deeply, as she felt he had been hurt.

Perhaps she surrendered because of this, knowing she would be hurt and haunted if he went away without her ; knowing in her heart that he didn't feel for her what he had felt for that other girl.

"Is it true that your house has a tower?"

"Do you like towers?" he asked drily.

"They're rather romantic."

"And you like what is romantic?"

'I'm almost afraid to answer that question ... you might think me naïve."

"Young, perhaps, but how could a nurse not know about life? When I look at you, Elvi, you seem never to have seen a birth or a dying, and I find it intriguing that my wife should have such an air of chastity ... only the flowers had it, until I met you."

"Y-you pay unusual compliments, Rodari." She felt the play of the evening wind against the warmth of her cheeks ... he knew her chaste, totally innocent of the demands of a man, and in so short a time they would arrive at his home and it would be their wedding night.

"You are a rare sort of girl and the usual sort of flattery would not be in keeping. Don't you like my compliments?"

"I'm unused to receiving them from a distinguished writer of best-selling novels."

"I am now your husband." His deep voice with its Latin accent seemed to infuse the words with extra meaning ... her husband, yet still a stranger in so many ways.

She could picture his home on its own *isola,* surrounded by olive groves and cypress trees, with lofty ceilings, wall frescoes and iron-work lanterns to light the vine-covered *terrazza* where they would dine and gaze out over the dark glimmer of the lake. In the distance would loom the mountains and down by the water among the ilex trees fireflies would glitter like tiny jewels.

She longed to see the place, and equally she feared to arrive there.

Elvi glanced at her husband and in the glow of the overhead light in the long dark car she saw the crease of amusement in his lean cheek. He sensed her alarm as they sped nearer all the time to the Isola Fortunato, and

14

as a man of sophistication he found it something to smile at, that unlike other women he had known she found him intimidating even though she wore his glimmering ruby ring. "Give me time to get used to you," she wanted to plead. But she knew in advance what his answer would be ... he would say that there was only one way for a bride to become accustomed to her husband.

Her heart beat fast as the car travelled downhill and the lights of a harbour came into view, illuminating the rigging of fishing sloops and those little hooped boats of Italian waters. There was a cluster of houses and sheds, a stone quay and the bounce of cobbles beneath their wheels as they drove along the quayside and came at last to a halt. The engine throbbed and then was stilled and Rodari turned in his seat to look at her for a long silent moment.

"We are now almost home," he said, and she saw a teasing quirk at the corner of his mouth. "You should be eager to see the island and the house, yet when I touch your hand you tremble, and when I speak to you as my *sposa* you look nervous. Do I look as if I plan to eat you ... like those tiny birds the Tuscans cook and sell, their tiny beaks open in a soundless plea, as your lips seem to be when I look at you?"

"You must remember that I'm far away from familiar things." She felt the lean strength of his fingers holding her wrist, the quick beating of her pulse beneath the pressure of his thumb. To be poised, to be assured, to know he cared deeply for her ... she would not behave like this if she were sure of his love.

"A nurses' home in Kensington?" he mocked softly. "Do you forget so soon, *cara,* that you told me you had only a stepmother after your own mother died and no real home any more to enjoy? A home is a precious thing to a woman. I give you one on an island, and another in Rome. What do you give me?"

Her heart felt as if like a bird it would break a wing ... with a desperate sort of shyness she put her arms around his neck and pressed her cold lips to his cheek. She could feel the thrust of his cheekbone and the hollow beneath it, and love for this stranger stirred her senses as they had never been before. Perhaps he would learn to love her as he had loved that other girl ... beautiful and wayward, Elvi guessed it even as she kissed his cheek. She dared not think how she would compete with that image in his heart. How she would compare with it in the days to come.

He smiled as his gaze passed over her, and a smoky fragrance clung to his coat as she leaned against his shoulder. "What an odd one you are," he murmured. "I wonder if I did right to pursue you? If you could have a wish, *neonata*, what would it be? Never to have met me?"

Even as she hesitated, too shy to voice the wish in her heart, someone swung a lantern beside the car and a voice spoke in Italian through the open window.

"Ah, our boatman!" Rodari exclaimed. "Manfredo, who will take us across to the island. Come, I am eager for you to see the house where I was born."

As they made their way to the boat Elvi saw gardens at the water's edge, like a little Venice. As their baggage was lowered to the boat a wind off the water tugged at her hair, and when she felt the hard grip of the boatman's hand she stepped down into the craft and took her seat. Rodari followed, the lanterns etching shadows into his face, and then the engine sprang to life and they were off.

The moon had risen and they sped across its silvery trails, breaking them into pieces and disturbing the night with the sound of their motor. No one spoke. Rodari seemed to savour his homecoming in a silence which held memories she could never share. The boatman concentrated on his steering, though now and again she was aware of his dark eyes upon her. Did he think her a dis-appointing wife for the *padrone*? A bit of a thing with a face too quiet for beauty, and eyes too serious for a bride?

She watched the island loom into view. The lake rolled around it like the sea itself, and the walls of the villa arose from the lake, overhung with cypress and oleanders, its slender towers and half-hidden windows giving the place a faintly sinister look.

Elvi's fingers clenched her purse and she thought of the Medici times, of duels and vendettas, and Dante's immortal love for Beatrice. The little windowpanes of the house were lit by the moon like the facets of dia-monds. There was a beauty and a mystery to the place that made her more aware than ever of her own lack of background and distinction. How would she cope as the mistress of the villa Fortunato and meet the demands of Rodari's life in Rome?

She closed her eyes in a silent prayer and when she opened them the boat was pulling in beside the landing stage, and Rodari and the boatman were talking to-gether in their rapid Italian. A few moments more and Elvi was standing on the island, gazing up at the villa where she was to spend her honeymoon. It was built on rock, with rambling walls giving it a fortified look, and steps had been hacked into the rock to form a rough stair-way overhung by a hedge of trees.

"Come!" Rodari took her hand, gripped it possessively and hurried her up the steps towards the lights of the villa. They passed beneath a tunnel of myrtle and cam-ellias, and the tree-frogs seemed to trill a welcome. She gave a gasp as a pale figure loomed, and then she heard the trickling sound of water and saw a statue of a nymph holding her draperies around a slim body. The water washed over the nymph and fell with a cool splash into the stone basin.

"Italian gardens are full of statues . . . in the moonlight

17

they seem to live again." Rodari brushed a trailing vine from their path. "Tomorrow I must show you the orchid house and our *kashmiri* cypress trees that turn to gold in the sunlight. We have also our own small chapel. My father and my mother were married there. She was a girl from a Tuscan peach farm and my father fought a long battle with his parents until at last they had to let her be his bride. Her name was Sabinetta, and whoever you meet on the island will tell you that she was more lovely than the peach blossom itself. She died when I was but a few days old. It has always annoyed my grand-mother in Rome that her son married a girl who liked to run about with bare feet and who could not conform to the rigid rules of Roman society in those days."

"I wonder what your grandmother will say when she meets me?" Elvi glanced up sharply as she felt the pain-ful tightening of his fingers, pressing the ruby ring into her hand so that she had to bite her lip or cry out.

"Do you run about with bare feet?" he jested.

"No . . . but I'm not exactly out of the top drawer, and the Contessa must have hoped that you would marry a girl of your own class."

"The Contessa will have to accept you instead, and though I warn you she is an autocratic old lady, my sister Elena is warm and kind. She is a widow. Her husband Flavio was mad about cars and he killed himself driving in a motor race. I wish she would marry again, but she clings to the memory of that wild boy to whom she was married so short a time. Love is a strange thing, Elvi. A strange and painful emotion which is best avoided."

Elvi took the first shock of his words in silence, then she reacted with sudden temper and pain. She wrenched her hand free of his and wouldn't enter the villa with him looking as if he couldn't bear not to have her close to him.

"What are you doing?" As swiftly as she broke free of him he took her by the shoulders and she found herself

18

pressed against a tree. A cloud of scent broke about her from the tight little flowers bunched on the branches, heady, dizzying, a part of the conflict smouldering between her and Rodari.

"Y-you can avoid me as well," she choked. "You can leave me alone and I'll go away tomorrow and you can forget you ever got entangled with a wife you don't happen to love. . . ."

"I married you because I need you." He shook her and petals from the flowers fell as softly as his words fell sternly. "I never pretended for one moment that I was a romantic boy, nor did I ask you to behave as if I were the lover of your dreams. We are two rather lonely people ... it was that we had in common. Believe me, Elvi, those vows we made today are not to be broken by a few words, a little anger, a speaking of the truth. With your lovely candid eyes you should prefer the truth to make-believe. You are real. I am real. This place is here for our honeymoon. There will be a honeymoon, make no mistake about that. You married me and there is no one on this island who will provide you with a boat against my orders."

"Y-you wouldn't give such an order!" she gasped.

"I would indeed, *neonata*. Why not? I am a Latin among my own people and we understand that a woman must be mastered."

"You talk as if you intend to make a – a prisoner of me!"

"Don't dramatise." He laughed softly, with a hint of mockery, and bent to kiss her lips. She turned her cheek, unable to forgive him for being so cruelly honest about his feelings, but there was no escaping him and with firmness he held her and made her surrender to his kiss. Her whole being cried out against it, and deliberately he caressed her throat in the opening of her fur coat, enclosing the slenderness of it in his lean hand as if he held a wine

19

chalice from which he took the sweet and bitter of her lips.

"You kiss me as if you offer yourself as a sacrifice," he taunted, and he betrayed his sense of ownership in the way he stroked the fur that framed her white throat and pale face, with the large eyes that seemed to dominate her other features. Grey eyes that in the shadows held the glitter of the tears she held forcibly in check. In her heart she could have cried a storm . . . she had thought it would suffice to love an unloving man, but now she knew how much it hurt to be only his possession.

"I kiss you to welcome you to the Villa Fortunato." A fine thread of steel ran through the words, as if he warned her not to try his Latin temper. "Surely after that long car journey you are glad to be here?"

She glanced about her as they mounted a curve of stone steps to the terrace. Beyond long windows lay a room firelit. The room seemed to slumber between the moon and the scent of woodsmoke, half dark, revealed slowly as her eyes grew accustomed to it. There was a certain enchantment, a certain menace, a half suggestion of secrets waiting to be revealed.

She gave a start as Rodari's hands closed hard on her shoulders. Her heart felt as if it would choke her with its fast beating, for he was surely going to lift her and carry her over the threshold, in the traditional way of a bridegroom with his bride. She tensed, waiting for it to happen, and then she heard him sigh.

"Let us go in," he said. "I felt you shiver when I touched you . . . go quickly to the fire and get warm."

She hesitated, and he propelled her forward. He was almost impatient with her . . . as if already he regretted his hasty marriage. She felt a compulsion to look at his face, to see if regret was written there, but if she saw it, the despair in his eyes, how would she live through the hours to come with any sort of joy in them?

"My dear," she could still hear that gossipy woman patient at the hotel, the stout one who had twisted her ankle trying to ski. "That man called Fortunato is the most attractive and intriguing creature. He has such dark and brooding eyes ... well, they say he was mad about some society beauty in Rome ... or was it Venice? Ah, Venice. Have you ever been there? Such a romantic place ... but then you nurses don't lead very romantic lives, do you?"

"Not very," Elvi had replied, while she made the plump ankle comfortable.

Was it on the rebound from her unromantic life that she had married Rodari?

"Come, don't dawdle," he said. "Or I shall think you are afraid of being alone with me."

"No ..." she said, but in her heart she was afraid.

CHAPTER II

THEY entered the beautiful, dusky room and Rodari pressed a switch and small crystal lamps came alight in shadowy corners and blue damask was revealed, and the sumptuous Italian furniture. Underfoot lay a vast carpet panelled with flowers.

He might not have been away for many weeks; everything was so shining and perfect, as if the master spent every day of his life at the villa. Every picture and ornament was exact in its place, but when Elvi turned to say how lovely was the room, she found Rodari's face a lean mask of severity. There was a steely click as he threw back the lid of a chased silver box and took a cigarette. The box was filled to the brim with the brand he always smoked, and the silver lighter beside it worked without a falter.

"It's a very charming room," Elvi said, for surely he demanded that she like this house built on a lake island.

"The *salotto grande*." He spoke through the smoke of his cigarette. "The room of the grand after-dinner gatherings of my grandmother's days, but we shall not have need of it. I don't intend to entertain anyone ... except my wife."

A tracery of smoke hung fine and blue about his dark head and his eyes seemed to smoulder as he looked at her. It was a look he had not given her before, and because it made her feel so intolerably shy, she glanced away from him and saw beyond his left shoulder a painting of a duellist dressed all in black. He stood there vividly, and arrogantly, in the great canvas, and a trick of the lamplight seemed to make his eyes as alive as Rodari's. The fragrance of good tobacco mingled with the scent of flowers in a porcelain vase.

"The house seems very quiet," she said, for only the murmuring of the fire and the ticking of the clock intruded when she and Rodari were not speaking. Any moment she had expected a tap on the door and the entrance of the woman who kept everything so in readiness for the *signorone*. Elvi dared a look at him. Why did no one come? Even the boatman had left after delivering their suitcases.

"I suppose I should have told you." Rodari spoke casually, but now he was standing beneath that portrait and the two men seemed as one, on guard though so apparently relaxed.

Elvi felt the beating of her heart as she waited for him to tell her why the house seemed to brood around them instead of offering a welcome.

"Delfina and her husband Dario never stay after dark. They go home to their house in the village, but as you can see we have a fire, our rooms upstairs will have been prepared for us, and there will be food all ready for eating."

Elvi stared at him and her heart beat nervously. "Why don't they stay?" She gave a little shiver and thought of the lake all around them, cutting them off for the night from the rest of the world. "Is the villa haunted?"

"Not really, but Italians are superstitious. Ever since my grandmother left the *isola* to go and live near Rome, the people of the village stay away from the Villa Fortunato."

"Why . . . what happened here, Rodari, to make them feel superstitious about the place?"

23

"It's because of the lake." He glanced towards the windows, as if he heard the water of the lake whispering in the night. "I never knew my mother . . . I had no chance to know her, because of the lake. She overheard my grandmother say that her baby must have the proper care of a nurse, in the Fortunato tradition, for mothers spoiled their children and it had to be remembered that Sabinetta was a Tuscan farm girl, reared to the idea that a child should be with its mother day and night."

Rodari paused and his profile was a Roman carving there against the moonlit glass of the window, stern with anger, and stony with the grief locked in his heart.

"Sabinetta heard all this through the nursery door, and though married to my father she was still the half-wild, impulsive girl who had run barefoot among the peach trees. She made up her mind that night to take her baby home to the farm, and when everyone was in bed she slipped from her bed, wrapped her baby son in a blanket and stole from the house down to the lakeside. She laid me on the shingle while she unhitched the boat, but someone heard her and came running to stop her. In panic she leapt into the boat, unaware that it was my father who called her, so afraid of my autocratic grandmother that she could think of nothing but getting away, certain she would be punished for trying to take her baby home with her. With her long auburn hair tangling in the wind she rowed the boat as far as her strength would take her. The heart of the lake is deep, holding cross-currents that come in from the sea. The currents gripped the boat and overturned it. My father swam out to save Sabinetta. She was barely alive when he reached the shore with her, and two days later she died of pneumonia. My father never ceased to miss her and died himself in the war."

Rodari walked to the fire, as if to seek its warmth. The end of his cigarette fell among the flames. "It all happened a long time ago, but since the villa stands unoccupied for most of the year the rumour has circulated that on moonlit nights the ghost of Sabinetta swims ashore in search of the son she wanted with her all the time."

"Rodari . . ." His name broke from Elvi, a plea that he stop hurting both of them by talking of the sad past. This was to be their honeymoon and already she must share him with the memory of another girl, and the ghost of his tragic young mother. She wanted to soothe away the ache in his heart, but she was only a girl herself and she wanted to be more than a means of forgetfulness.

"You look all eyes when you look at me," he said. "Do you mind, *mia cara,* that I brought you here? Did you wish for crowds when we can have this small island to ourselves?"

"Sometimes in a crowd, Rodari, two people can lose themselves more easily."

"More easily than among the shapes of memories and their whispers. Come!" He reached out and gripped her hand. "I will show you the room in which Delfina will have laid our wedding supper. Strange, eh, that I should love this house as much as I hate it?"

"Love and hate are twin souls," she said, and there was no escaping his touch, or the mastery of his smile . . . the smile whose hint of melancholy had made her love him before she realised how much wiser she would have been to leave Italy. Only by putting mountains and the sea between them would she have been safe from the dark caressing glance that could also be a little cruel.

They left the drawing-room and passed through a small foyer with a striking male statue standing alone on a marble floor, the strong body draped by a cloak over the shoulder and the left arm. Apollo, she thought, the sun god who pursued the nymph.

"Here we are." He ushered her into a small room that came as a delightful shock after the serene formality of the *salotto.* It was arched over with a dome patterned with stucco birds. A round amber lamp hung on a chain, and a table was set for a meal on a low table in front of a halfmoon sofa. The firelight shone on chafing dishes ready to be lit. Wine and fruit made a soft glow of colour. And on a dish of fine blue china lay a small mound of sugar-coated almonds, the traditional sweets of an Italian wedding.

"Shall we eat now?" Rodari asked. "Or would you like to go upstairs and change your dress?"

"What would you like to do?" She gave him a shy smile, for the little domed room had eased her feeling of tension. It seemed set aside for midnight trysting; a small sanctuary with no ancestral faces to watch from the walls.

"I should like you to wear the velvet dress we shopped for in Rome. It will make the occasion more festive."

"The Florentine velvet," she murmured. "You insisted upon buying it, but a dress like that is really meant for a seductive beauty."

"You have bewitching eyes, *madonnina*." He drew her to him and kissed her eyes. "They have a shining tranquillity like the dove-grey velvet, with a hint of intriguing violet. Such a dress should be worn on the eve of a marriage."

At once he made her acutely aware that tonight was no ordinary night in her life. For better or worse she had entwined her life with his and must await happiness or disaster.

They went upstairs, passing panelled walls hung with framed portraits of the Fortunato men and women. Some of the men were handsome but severe; the women were dressed in forgotten styles, but there seemed to linger in their eyes a gleam of joy in having married a Fortunato, or a shadow of regret.

Elvi looked at each portrait with interest, but she waited in vain for her husband to say: "This was my mother." She looked at the framed faces of children, but he didn't say: "That was me when I was a boy."

In a little corner gallery with a balustrade overlooking the hall he paused in front of a pair of portraits and when he spoke his voice was stern. "My grandparents," he said. "The Contessa still lives, as you know, and having ruled the lives of her family most of her life she tries to rule mine. I look forward to the moment when I confront her with my English wife. She hoped, and ordered, an Italian woman of rank for my *sposa*. La Contessa has a jolt in store for her."

His words frightened Elvi. She wanted to be liked and accepted by his family, but he spoke as if he hoped his choice of a bride would upset them.

"Did you marry me, Rodari, as a sort of revenge?" she asked.

His eyes blazed into hers, then softened, but dangerously. "No man would take such a drastic step for the sake of sweet revenge, though I do find you sweet, *mia cara,* when you look at me with defiance in your eyes and a tinge of your natural compassion. Is it the man I am, or the boy I was, that excites your compassion?"

"I don't know," she said. "You are still a mystery to me." Still the man who that first night at the alpine hotel had stood alone on the terrace while the other guests sang together around a blazing log fire to the music of a concertina and chestnuts bursting in their skins at the edge of the flames. She had been on duty with a patient and had come downstairs to fetch a glass of milk and a slice of cake, passing him by without being seen by him. A lean and lonely man; a graceful matador shadow in the night, his dark head sheened by the many stars that hung like golden spiders on the webbing of the sky.

"No two people on the threshold of a new life together should know too much about each other." He took her hand, pressing the ruby into her finger as he led her to the door of her room. He opened the door and switched on

27

the light, and she turned her eyes swiftly from the crown-shaped canopy and long silken shape of a bed too big for one person.

"My dressing room is through that connecting door," he said, and there was a slight drawl to the words, as if he had noticed not without amusement that swift retreating look she had given the fourposter that dominated the bedroom.

"And the bathroom?" she enquired, fighting to sound composed.

An adjoining door led into it, with a deep mosaic bath let into the floor, a gleam of Italian tile, long mirrors, and flagons. The villa was a fascinating blend of the old with the new, and being a practical as well as an imaginative person Elvi could appreciate both aspects.

"What luxury," she murmured. "A shower stall as well."

"At least you will have no regrets about the practical side of our marriage," he said. "My apartment in Rome is situated in a restored *palazzo* overlooking the Tiber."

"Who would have thought of Nurse Lloyd in surroundings so smart?" She smiled, but it ached a little on her mouth. Luxury was nice, but she would have sacrificed it all to possess his love.

With a sudden adroit movement he spun her towards him. "You are now my wife, the Signora Elvina Fortunato. Who thought to call you Elvina? It goes strangely well with my name."

"Why aren't you called the Conte Fortunato?" she asked.

"Would you like to be a Contessa?" His smile was mocking. "I have no use for titles, much to my grandmother's indignation. I dropped the title from my name when I became a writer. I wanted to succeed as an individual, not as part of a dynasty."

"You are very headstrong, Rodari."

"Of course." His teeth gleamed white against his dark

28

skin. "We have always been a family of strong passions. Our desires are as strong as our hates, and we never forgive very easily. La Contessa was never kind to my mother, though strangely enough she has always idolised Elena, my sister, who is a year older than I. It could be that she took Elena from my mother without a fight. When a son was born Sabinetta wanted him more fiercely . . . Italian women live to have a son."

He made the word sound intolerably significant. "Elvi." As he spoke her name she felt the caress of his hand down the side of her neck to her shoulder. "I wonder if you will give me a son."

Her blush seemed to cover half her body. Only a Latin husband could say such a thing to a girl newly married; an Englishman would have been talking about the promising warmth of the weather and what should they do to pass the time. She had never blushed all over before, and she wanted to run and hide from the man who could make upon her every claim justified by the marriage laws of Rome. The candles had burned bright on the altar until towards the end of the ceremony one of them had flickered and cast a shadow.

She looked at him now as she remembered looking at him in the chapel, with the candle flames dancing their shadows over the haunting bone structure of his face. Then as now she had thought him as lean and imperious as a Medici lord, a man born to make demands, born to be loved with a half-frightened love.

"Don't look at me like that." A smile flickered at the edge of his mouth. "There is time for everything, and I must remember that you are an English girl who had a career before I came along."

"A very useful one, Rodari. I suppose now I must give it up?"

"Of course, *cara*." He spoke decisively. "You now have a husband and a home to look after, and that husband grows hungry and would like his supper in a short while."

He left her alone in the bedroom, where she unpacked the dress he wished her to wear and laid it across the bed. She took from its box the silk lingerie made by the nuns who could never wear it, even if they longed to in their secret hearts.

What would her friends at the nurses' home have to say if they could see her now, the fair and slender Nurse Lloyd with the quiet grey eyes that made her patients feel they could trust her? She glanced around her at the Italian furniture with mother-of-pearl inlay, and heard the soft chiming of the clock with the porcelain pendants. Here in this strange, handsome room she would spend the coming night with Rodari, who without saying once that he loved her had persuaded her to become his wife.

Had the need for sweet revenge driven him? The Contessa had hoped he would marry an Italian woman . . . Elvi felt certain he had loved one, but something had gone wrong, and whoever that woman was she would meet in future a man who was married.

Elvi stared at herself in a mirror whose carved frame of tiny imp faces and flowers seemed to emphasise the fact that she was a girl who was very English and out of place in this Italian room. Her skin was rose-white and flawless. Her mouth was shy, but could curve quickly into a smile of humour. Her eyes were almost too large, and her hair was cut pageboy style. Few people would have called her plain, but few men would have turned to stare at her.

"Why, Rodari?" she whispered. "Why me?"

She came downstairs wearing the Florentine velvet, and she seemed hardly able to support the weight of the material and held the full skirt with her hands. From the hem came the glint of her silver slippers, and around her curved the black and gold staircase. Now she felt and looked more like a bride, a rather medieval one, perhaps, on her way to meet a bridegroom who in looks and attitudes was of another time, the old days of vendettas and roast peacock. She reached the foot of the stairs and paused to get her bearings, a hand reaching to the black newel post and gripping it until her ring gleamed like fire or blood against the dark wood.

The house was very quiet, all she could hear was the wind playing around its walls. Everything was very still, except for the slight movement of the long velvet curtains at the windows along the hall.

"Rodari . . ." His name formed on her lips as she looked about for him. She had heard him leave the dressing-room some time before, and told herself with a faintly self-derisive smile that he was probably in the dome room pouring their wine and that she had nothing to fear from the sad ghost of Sabinetta. Like Sabinetta she loved him and wanted to be with him.

She crossed the hall, her reflection in the Florentine dress catching and holding in the mirrors that broke the dark panelling of the walls. Lamps were enclosed in black wrought-iron, casting around her a strange halo of light. Her shoulders draped by the cowl line of the dress were very slim and white, and she wondered what he would think of her as she opened the door of the dome room and went inside. She expected at once to see Rodari and it came as a shock to find the small, charming room quite empty of his tall presence.

Where could he be? She walked slowly to the fireplace and the scent of the cypress logs was like an incense, reminding her again of the chapel where they had vowed to love and cherish each other. She knelt on the rug and there was in the way she held her hands to the warmth almost a sort of supplication. Each spurt of the flames, each tiny rustle of her skirt added to the sense of silence

31

... and desertion. She gazed sombrely into the warm heart of the fire, and cold were her thoughts. If a man cared anything at all for a girl, then he didn't leave her alone to wonder and wait, and to hear in every small sound the suggestion of a ghostly footfall.

Sabinetta, said the people of the *isola,* swam ashore on moonlit nights seeking the son other people had taken away from her. Now in a way Elvi had taken him, and she glanced around nervously, wondering if in her lifetime the girl from the peach farm had sat alone in this curious and delightful room.

Had she loved a man of whom she was terribly unsure? A man of tempered charm and arrogance, who felt that his wife should let him have his own way in everything?

This she was puzzling over when the curtains suddenly billowed at the windows and were parted by a lean hand, dark-skinned against the ruby material. With a little cry of surprise Elvi jumped to her feet and watched as like a cloak the curtains swung into place behind her husband. He wasn't smiling, and his black hair was wet and yet rough about the dark chiselling of his Italian face. A towel swung from his other hand, and the heavy white silk of his shirt was open against the brown chest with its wing of dark hair. A small cross on a chain gleamed against his skin, and long narrow trousers made his legs seem even longer as he came slowly across the room to where she stood, velvet-clad in the lamplight. Lamps with small golden shades that distilled a soft radiance.

Rodari stared down at her and it was as if he had brought the night in with him and the glitter of the lake, caught between the black eyelashes.

"You look as if you came from another century," he said. "Tonight, my dear, you are a rare enchantress."

She heard him, yet the words and their meaning were lost when she looked at him. He had been swimming in the lake, unafraid of the ghosts of Fortunato island. He had been there in the black and silver flecked water, and he returned to her looking like a Byronic corsair.

"I-I'm glad you like the dress," she said. "I feel very grand in it, but as if I'm masquerading as someone other than myself."

"Shall I join the masquerade?" he asked, a smile at the edge of his mouth. "What shall be my guise, Elvi?"

"You need none," she replied. "You look already as if you had been out plundering the seas for pieces of eight."

"A pirate, eh?"

"Most definitely."

"Shall I see if my loot contains something to go with that ravishing dress?"

He spoke English words flawlessly, but with an accent that made some of them take on extra meaning. She felt the colour steal into her cheeks when he used the word ravishing. "I – I don't want you to keep giving me things. Please, Rodari –"

"Please," he mocked. "You are the only woman I know who makes the word sound not a plea but a prayer. Never tell a man not to give you presents, especially if that man is the one who has the right to give, and to take."

"I have given you so little," she said.

"The leather stud-box I like very much, and you forget," he dwelt on the words, "that in marriage a woman gives herself."

He took and held her gaze with his own, and she felt the power and assurance of him in every single nerve of her body. The heavy white silk of his shirt clung to his damp skin and moulded the muscles of his chest and shoulders. He looked dangerously vital and foreign and she couldn't help but wonder if he would be a savage lover. Fear must have leapt into her eyes, for his laugh was savage as he strode to the door. "Serve the food," he called back. "I shall not keep you waiting."

She went to the table and used a cloth to lift the lids from the chafing-dishes simmering over the little blue flames. There was asparagus in a butter sauce. Mushrooms and quail in a wine sauce. Crisp veal and vegetables, and a beautifully cut and arranged fruit salad. The food smelled good, and with the absorbed care and pleasure of the new housewife Elvi arranged the plates, and admired the wine glasses. They were Venetian, she thought, with slender stems and fluted bowls. She flicked a fingernail against one of them and the crystal made a soft and lingering note. She touched the sumptuous dark red roses in the long-stemmed vases. She gazed at the sweet-coated almonds that were rarely missing from the table of a newly married couple in Tuscany.

The door opened and she felt herself going tense again. It wasn't easy loving Rodari. He was like love itself, an invader, a bringer of strange thoughts and mysterious emotions.

"We are fortunate, Elvi. We have wine and food and no one but ourselves to worry about." As he came to her he gave the table, the log fire, the closed curtains, a rapid glance, and he smiled as if he enjoyed the thought of having her so completely to himself. She had never loved before, or felt like this before, and she couldn't have said which feeling came uppermost . . . fear or fascination.

"Long ago an ancestor of mine must have plundered a convent for this." The trinket gleamed in his lean hands, a pearl rosary hung with a single lustrous ruby. It was lovely, virginal, and yet the ruby added a touch of passion. Elvi was in his hands and the rosary was fastened about her neck, and for a brief, intolerably tense moment she felt close to her the darkness and strength of this man who distilled a disturbing magic that could not be called love . . . love as she had believed it to be.

It was after all pearls and rubies, things of purity and passion. She felt passion in his touch, and the shock of

34

her own need for this tall stranger she had married. It made her pull away from him, and with a careless laugh he turned to the table and drew out a chair for her. He was not insisting on a response right now: the food awaited them.

He sat down facing her and he poured their Tuscan wine from the decanter traced with silver. He liked lovely things about him, and Elvi wondered what his thoughts were as he shared with her the quail and the grapes, and the sugared almonds. Was he remembering another face, another voice, a woman who had possessed the grace of long-stemmed roses; a beauty perhaps as maddening as Rodari's *savoir rien*.

Perhaps he read her thoughts, for he began to talk of Italy and the places they would see together. Rome, mellowed by the sun of centuries, where men with faces like Rodari had raced chariots along the Appian Way, and in other times had stalked the streets of Florence with a cloak flaring from wide shoulders, the gleam of a rapier at the lean hip. He was Italian to his bones; the finest and most subtle blood ran in his veins. He reminded her of a gothic angel she had seen in a chapel; he could be incredibly gracious, but there slumbered in his dark eyes the fires of devilry.

He had said of her, almost at their first meeting, that she possessed the quality known in Italy as *gentilezza*.

"You have much heart," he said, and he proceeded to steal most of it. If she reserved a small quarter of her heart, it was in self-defence. She must never let herself forget that someone else had stolen Rodari's heart.

"We are perfect here," he said. "Remote and by ourselves. You can't know, *cara,* how good it feels to get away from people. I see so many when a film is in progress and I am there to watch the procedure."

She listened to him speaking in that accented voice that made the English language new and exciting. She

35

noticed how the antique glass he held blended with the ruthless beauty of the lean hand that carried no ring. His only jewellery was a gold-faced watch on a leather strap, and his cuff-links were set with a single dark stone. He was not a man who flashed his wealth in self-adornment, but he always wore suits of impeccable tailoring.

He talked of the lemon groves that were set around the island like the hanging gardens of Babylon. Sometimes everything was golden, with the sun on the lake and the hanging fruit and the lemon flowers. Then in the olive groves the world turned silver.

"You will remember your honeymoon," he said. "I intend that you should."

He rose to his feet and switched on the radiogram. Music played, a song she knew but whose words were evasive as a perfume remembered from another time. Arms enclosed her and she danced with Rodari to the music of a forgotten song.

"Do you know the words?" he asked.

"No, but I remember they were sad."

"Sadness is always a part of beauty." He held open the *terrazza* curtains and they stepped out into the black and silver shadows. The wide cream cups of the magnolias glimmered along the wall, brimming with shadow. The moon was half in, half out of a cloud, and Elvi stared at the broken moon and hoped it wasn't a portent of trouble to come.

"Look up there and you will become moon-witched." Rodari took her chin in his fingers and made her look at him. "There is something romantic and suffering about grey eyes, and you have a curve to your lashes. They are the eyes of a young nun. They look at me with such candour, and yet with a hint of fear. They ask a hundred questions of me, and I can't answer any of them at this time. I can only tell you, *mia cara,* that tonight I want no one but you. If someone came this moment and tried to

36

take you away, then I think I would turn murderous."

"Rodari," her voice shook slightly, but she had to speak now the words that had been in her mind all the evening, "*signore,* what if I asked you . . . please, would you give me time to get used to you?"

"Be more specific." He spoke quietly enough, but there was an underlying flick of the lash that made Elvi clench nervously the stonework of the terrace wall. In the night air the trees stirred, and a cigale trilled without pause in the moonlight, and fireflies tangled in the hanging vines. The lake far below was fired to silver, and there was heartbreak in the beauty of the scene. It was made for those in love, but Rodari wished for the forgetfulness which passion brings.

"Y-you know what I mean. You understand me," she said.

"I only know, my dear, that today I married you, and tonight I make you my wife."

"Please . . . is it so much to ask? A little time in which to become more used to you?"

"The best way to know me is in my arms." His fingers toyed with the pearl rosary and the ruby . . . a lover's stone. "You are not a coy person, only a rather shy one . . ."

"No . . ." She broke away from him, and as she did so the clasp of the pearl rosary broke apart and like a milky streak with fire in it the rosary went flying over the wall of the *terrazza* to the rocks below the villa. There was an awful silence, and then with an Italian curse on his lips Rodari took hold of her and swung her up into his arms.

"Tomorrow we will search for the rosary!"

"The tide will wash it into the water!"

"Which will be a pity, but not such a great one that I intend to go down now with a hand torch to hunt for the necklace." He held her grey eyes with his, his face in

37

shadow except for the dark glinting eyes. "Did you hope I might?"

"It's an heirloom, and we could search together."

"I shall look for your pearls just before the dawn tide. You will awake wearing them, *carina.*"

There was no misunderstanding him, no escape from the demanding eyes, the breath that stirred warm across her lips, the feel of steel in the arms of this man who had her so alone and at his mercy at the Villa Fortunato.

His lips closed on hers, drawing them half open, like the invaded petals of a flower. She gave a sharp little moan, for his kiss of impatient desire held the promise of pain. Frightened, she beat at him, hurting her hands against him. "I shall hate you," she cried.

"Will you, *mia cara?* I wonder." There was a half-mocking laughter in his kiss, and the moonlight was left behind them, replaced by the glimmer of the hall lamps. He trod the stairs with a panther silence and swiftness, striding with her past the gaze of the Fortunato family, forever watchful in the upward curving line of portraits. He carried her into their bedroom, and impatient now of the Florentine velvet and the cobweb silk woven by the nuns, he was brutal with the hidden zip, the lacy straps, the slender body white against the madonna blue of the bedspread. She felt the lean strong hands, the lips that burned her skin. Her cry of capture was lost in his warm lips.

"I shall hate you . . ." she had cried, but as the moonlight lay broken on the dark floor, she could only cling and hold and let him find his forgetfulness.

It wasn't hate she felt at all . . . only a sudden, fainting rapture.

CHAPTER III

SHE would never know a wilder fire than this . . . so were her thoughts during the nights and days which followed. Days spent beneath an Italian sky, exploring this island of lemons, of fishing craft with flared sails, and small houses white-hot in the sun. A sunlight that shone from the moment it crept in past the shutters of the villa to become a blazing invader that filled the courtyards with the clamour of cicadas and the green of lizards, turned to a stone stillness upon the steps and walls that wended downwards to the shore.

A red ribbon bound her hair, its tails like a scarlet butterfly as she ran down the rough stone steps to meet her husband. He had been out with one of the boats. The *padrone* who liked to mingle with the island folk so he could listen to their tales and their troubles and find material for his own work.

There he stood, a basket of giant prawns and crabs at his feet, lounging against a palmetto with the smoke of a cheroot drifting about his dark, sea-tousled head. He wore an open shirt and fishing jeans, yet still he retained an air of raffish distinction.

It was a blue and silver morning, and still very early. He never slept late, or retired until midnight. He had boundless physical energy, and Elvi knew that he prowled the villa gardens late at night because he was restless for something . . . was it still that other woman?

His gaze brooded upon the water as she approached him. If he heard her steps across the shingle he didn't turn his head. He seemed this morning in the mood to let her know that his thoughts were far away, beyond this island they had shared and which she had grown to love.

She watched his profile with its trace of melancholy, alone in the depth of his thoughts with the sun slashing through a palm frond to mark his face with gold. How she loved, and feared, this man who was lover and stranger at the same time. She paused and stood very still, by nature unobtrusive and not wishing to intrude. The scent of wild herbs filled the sunlit air, a dark butterfly chased a blue one, and with fluttering wings they were lost behind the green and purpled vine that trailed over a wall.

She stared as if transfixed, for nature seemed to emphasise the fact that the strong could overwhelm the weak, and she gave a painful start as a lizard snapped its jaws on something bright and moving.

"You are much too sensitive, *carina*." The words came drawlingly from Rodari. "Life is a jungle and love is a hunger, and you must not be shocked by either, or let it hurt you too much."

"Have I shown signs of being shocked?" she asked, hoping she sounded as brave and gay as the ribbon that tied her hair like a bunch of ripe corn.

He flicked his eyes over her face, and then with a faintly teasing smile he reached out and drew her to his side. "Don't ever try to be a woman of the world. It would never suit you, and you suit me as you are."

"Shy and gauche? Someone the island folk look at as if she's a child you adopted instead of the woman you married. Do they believe we're married?"

"I should hope so." He gave her a look that brought the quick colour storming into her cheeks. "You have such a look of innocence in those large grey eyes that automatically I could be the rake who has snatched you from your playpen, but the island people know me, and after a month with you, Elvi, I begin to know you. Shall I kiss you?"

"Please . . . no."

"When you plead with me I want very much to kiss you."

"I haven't had my breakfast. I waited for you, hoping we might go to that little place where they cook anchovies on the charcoal and serve them with that delicious brown bread and coffee."

"Little gourmet! You are learning how to select the best food from the sham, eh? You are becoming quite a student of good living since I made you mine."

"Rodari," she gave a breathless laugh, "you say it so possessively, as if you bought me for a pet who must learn to be cute for your smart friends in Rome."

"Nonsense." He took her corn-bright hair in his fist and swung it like a tassel. "I want you to appreciate the refinements of living, that is all. I don't want you to lose your essential warmth. If you became just a toy," his fingers tightened on her hair and he drew her head back until his gaze fastened on her lips, "then I should be tempted to break you."

Her heart raced, a wild thing inside her, as his hands slipped down her body and he clasped her waist and held her against him. Her soft mouth suffered the aggression of his. "Always," he whispered, "you will have virginal eyes and a loving mouth. These I want. Deny me ever and I shall turn savage."

"Y-you would never allow me to deny you."

"You speak of our wedding night?"

"Yes."

"Did you hate me as much as you believed you would?"

"No."

"You awoke wearing the rosary as I promised. The pearls lay soft against your skin, and I think I shall always remember you like that."

He touched her neck where the pearls had lain, the ruby burning darkly in the hollow of her shoulder. She shivered at his touch, a delight and a terror, something that could sweep her into his possession until the pillars of the world came tumbling down. Then there was no memory of the shy and lonely nurse she had been, going quietly and efficiently about her duties. Then there was only Rodari, his hard arms around her as she fell asleep, to awake to the sunlight thrusting into their lake-scented room. She often woke alone, just as she lay alone, until he came to her from his restless wandering around the gardens of the villa. It was as if she stilled the memories for him when he took her into his arms. He was never cruel, but he never said he loved her. In the darkness, a little heart-bruised, she would feel like crying. And then he would cradle her against his chest and she would feel his breathing as he fell asleep. He thrilled her young, unawakened senses, but each day with him, each night that followed, she wanted his love more and more. She wanted to be the only girl he had ever truly loved.

As if reading her mind he said against her earlobe: "We are *simpatico*. What else should we need?"

"Breakfast," she said gaily.

He laughed and swung the basket of shellfish over his shoulder. "We will take an offering to Cesare and he will give us grass of light to eat with our anchovies."

"Wine, at this time of the day?"

"Italians are a warm-hearted people because they drink wine not at the accustomed hour but whenever they feel in good spirits."

"Is that how you feel, Rodari?"

"Yes, at the moment. Happiness is not always with one, like one's nose, but right now I could toss you to the other shoulder and carry you up the hill. Shall I do so?"

"No, thanks." She ran ahead of him up the grassy slope

that led to the quaint old café with sun-peeled shutters and rickety tables set in a garden overrun by fruit trees. The place had seen better days, but Cesare the owner had never lost his knack with seafood. Most visitors to the island found their way at some time to the café on the hilltop.

Cesare had a granddaughter who was talked about on the island. She had run away to Rome, where she had fallen in love with a rogue and had a baby. Cesare had never closed his doors to her and Nicolina had come home a few weeks before, bringing her baby with her, and it always troubled Elvi to see the girl sitting under the trees rocking the cradle and looking so withdrawn. She never left the café, and she never spoke to anyone. Whenever Elvi entered the garden with Rodari, the girl would gaze at them with enormous dark eyes, and if Rodari looked at her, she would bend her head and look like a young madonna at her penance.

Today Cesare was looking worried. Nicolina seemed to be pining after the devil who had taken her good name. Could the *padrone* help in any way? Would he talk to the foolish girl and make her see sense? She was home again and safe, and in time the islanders would forget and accept her again as one of them. After all, these things happened, and the *padrone* was a man of the world.

Rodari frowned, and then he spoke abruptly to Elvi. "It might be a good idea if you spoke to her. You are both of an age, and you may be able to convince her that life is not over because of one mistake. Tell her she will meet someone else . . . someone who will be nicer to her."

Elvi gave him an uncertain look. "Go with Cesare," he insisted. "You must learn as my wife to deal with awkward situations."

"Very well," she arose from the table and followed Cesare to his granddaughter's room, where she found the girl weeping on her bed. The baby lay crying as well, and Elvi picked him up, found he needed a change of diaper and proceeded to change him. He was olive-skinned, with black curly hair and eyes of brown made extra appealing by the long, tear-clustered lashes. Powdered and made comfortable, he nuzzled Elvi with his curly head, and she played with him and waited for Nicolina to stop feeling so sorry for herself.

At last the girl sat up and wiped the tears from her face with her hand. She stared resentfully at Elvi, and said something she obviously believed the English girl would not understand. But Elvi had studied Italian before taking her job in the Alps, and conversations with Rodari were proving a big help. He wanted her to speak his language fluently and she was proving a ready pupil.

"Don't call me smug," she reproved Nicolina. "I know what a crazy emotion love is, and how it can take a girl unaware. I know it can be hurtful."

"You have a ruby ring on your finger, *signora*. You have made the big match with the *padrone* of the island, but you don't really know what Italian men are like. They are clever at getting round a girl, but when that girl is in trouble they are quick to stay away from her." Nicolina slid off the bed, revealing the well-shaped brown limbs of a nymph. She had been too pretty, perhaps. Now her eyelids were swollen, her lips were sullen, and her joy in living had turned bitter. She took her baby from Elvi's arms, and as she did so she flicked her eyes over the English girl.

"I think he would give much, the distinguished and good-looking *padrone,* to have a son like mine. I wonder if he will, from a wife so pale-skinned and delicate? Did you know that he loved someone else? He brought her to the *isola* a year ago this month . . . I was then in Rome, but I heard that she looked like a *contessa* camellia in the garden of the villa. Later on she married someone else. She had been this other man's *fidanzata* from a young

44

girl and the alliance could not be broken ... but they say on the island that the heart of the *signorone* was broken."

When the girl ceased to speak there was a tense little silence, and then Elvi seemed driven to her feet, as if by a blow. Expected all along as it was, the revelation came as a shock. Though this embittered girl never left the café, people came to it. They talked and in the shade of the trees Nicolina listened. If she meant to shake Elvi, then she succeeded. If she meant to hurt her, then she was rewarded by the whiteness of Elvi's face when she said:

"You have a fine baby boy. Take care of him and don't be too unhappy. You are very pretty, Nicolina. You will find love again."

She left the room and went downstairs. She rejoined Rodari in the garden, where he was being shown the art of grilling the fat anchovies over the charcoal fire. It was like a ritual, and Elvi pretended to be far more interested than she was. Her real thoughts were not on food, for gone was the appetite she had arrived with. She could only think of the woman who had looked as lovely as a *contessa* camellia. It was she whom Rodari had loved and admired. Everyone knew that Elvi was second choice ... his bride at random. That was why everyone spoke to her as if she were plain and gauche. They had seen the other woman in the *padrone's* life, so beautiful and assured, but bound to marry a man chosen for her long before she met Rodari.

It was cruel, a procedure left over from stern Victorian times, the arranging of a marriage between a couple. In upper-class Italy it still went on. The blending of blue blood and money. The betrothal of a young girl to an elderly man.

Elvi caught her breath. How Rodari would have hated it if the girl he loved had let herself be married to a man

45

much older than herself. That would make him bitter. That would induce him to take his sweet revenge by marrying someone lots younger than himself, and poor.

He turned to look at her as Cesare served the food. "You had a satisfactory talk with the girl?"

"Yes, we talked, but I don't really know whether I helped her. It's hard to help anyone who has been hurt by loving someone too much."

"Can anyone be loved too much?" he asked, looking quizzical.

She bent her head to her plate and pretended not to have heard him. The crisp anchovies were delicious, but she had to force them down. The soft white wine in the rough glasses helped a little to dispel her sense of gloom. Rodari mustn't guess or know that she had been given a haunting description of the woman he had loved. What was more lovely than to be likened to a camellia?

"The other morning you ate like a starved urchin." Rodari reached out, took her chin between his fingers and make her look at him. "Has it made you unhappy to speak with that foolish girl?"

"It's men who make girls behave foolishly. Afterwards they don't want to know. They get away with everything."

"You mean we sin and never pay?"

"Yes, sinning is easier for a man."

"Do you wish it were easier for a woman?"

"Of course not, but why are people so hard towards a girl who has done wrong? She can't do so without the help of a man, yet no one treats a man like an outcast. He can swagger off to his next conquest while the poor girl brings up his child and pines for a bit of friendship and understanding from her neighbours. I feel sorry for Nicolina. Perhaps if she had been less pretty that brute in Rome might have left her alone."

"Perhaps she would not leave him alone. Had you thought of that?"

"In most cases the man does the chasing."

"How unworldly you are!" Rodari lifted his wine glass and laughed mockingly. "Because you would never chase after a man yourself, you can't conceive of any other girl doing so. But they do, *mia*. They often ask for trouble, and if the man is scornful afterwards who can really blame him?"

"You pretend to be so cynical." Elvi looked straight at him. "In your heart you don't believe what you have just said. I would know, Rodari, and I wouldn't be sitting here with a selfish man. You're proud and fiery and relentless about somethings, but you aren't a man who lives only for himself."

"*Grazie*." He tossed back his wine, and when he replaced the glass on the table there was a sudden devastating charm to his smile. "I had no idea that I had been married for my virtues. Are you sure I have them, or are you clinging to a romantic dream?"

"Nurses are not romantic people. They see too much suffering."

"Then what made you marry me?"

"I – I became fond of you."

"Only fond?" His dark gaze roved her fair-skinned face that showed a blush too clearly. As her cheeks grew pink, the depth of his eyes seemed to fill with glimmers of possessive amusement. She was his to tease, his to touch, his to make happy or sad. He seemed to revel in the love he had made her feel for him. She belonged to him alone, and he was letting her know it.

Unable to bear that look that owned her, she followed the flight of a ruby-tiger across the old herb garden with its trees like cloisters. And it was then she saw the flash of a blue skirt at the brink of the cliffs. She stared, and then had an awful premonition of what was about to happen. Nicolina had been wearing blue . . . it was she who stood there staring down at the water of the lake, another wild and pretty creature who was desperately unhappy.

"Rodari . . . that girl is going to jump!"

Elvi was on her feet as she spoke and darting among the trees towards the cliff edge. Her husband passed her, almost thrusting her out of his path, and a few seconds later the girl could be seen struggling with him at the cliff edge. Suddenly, in front of Elvi's eyes, the ground gave way beneath the feet of Nicolina and her husband, and they plunged out of sight down the steep rocky slope to the water. Elvi screamed and seemed for a moment to be turned to stone. Then she was hurling herself at the cliff, uncaring that more land might slide away, frantic to see if Rodari had been hurt.

By some miracle he was in the water and he was holding the girl by the shoulders and hauling her to the shore. Her long hair could be seen plainly, dragging her head back and revealing her white, senseless face.

"Thank God!" Elvi breathed the words and clutched the torn roots and grass where the cliffs had broken. She knew that if Rodari had struck his head on a rock, he and the girl would have drowned.

As it was Nicolina was unconscious for several hours and had cuts on her brown limbs. Elvi looked after her, and grew fond of the baby Nico.

It was on the fourth day, while she was tidying Nicolina's room while she rested in the garden, that Elvi found the typewritten note beneath the pillow. It was much-folded as if it had been read over and over again, and at the bottom of it there was a single initial, a bold R.

Elvi didn't mean to read the note, but somehow the words leapt at her. *We cannot meet any more. What we had is now over, and I have put cash into the bank for you so you will be financially secure for a long time to come. It has been fun and you have been someone I needed at an unhappy time in my life. This goodbye is inevitable, believe me. I told you from the beginning*

48

*that I could never marry you. You said you understood.
R.*

It was a note from a man who was trying to be kind.
A man who had enjoyed the liaison but was now cutting
free of it. Elvi flinched; she could imagine the shock to
the girl, who must have lovingly hoped that her lover
would in the end legalise their union. Instead he had put
money in the bank for her and written his goodbye on a
typewriter.

Elvi refolded the note, and that bold, slashing R
seemed to dance in her brain. She thought of the baby
Nico with his black curly hair and his brown eyes deep in
lashes. She relived that moment when her husband had
struggled with the girl on the cliff edge. He had said
something to her. What was it? Why couldn't she remember? She thrust her fingers against her temples and tried
to force the words out of her memory.

It was no use. The shock of seeing the cliffside breaking
away had driven the words completely from her mind,
but she was almost certain that Rodari had cried out
some intimacy, and his arms had held the girl as they fell
together.

She gave a cold little shiver, and then pulled herself
together and proceeded with her bedmaking. It was madness to believe that Rodari had been the girl's lover and
was the father of her child, yet the initial was the same
as his, and regardless of his own safety he had saved Nicolina's life. He was also rich enough to be able to settle a
considerable sum on the girl, if she was on his conscience.

All at once the small white-walled room seemed unbearably hot and too intimately redolent of the perfume
used by the Italian girl. The Madonna in her wall niche
seemed to gaze too sadly at Elvi, whose mind seethed
with questions. She hastened from Nicolina's bedroom,
closing the door firmly behind her. She wanted to gulp
at the fresh air outside, and then to be gone from the café

where only a few days ago she had so enjoyed breakfast in the old cloistered garden where lovers down the years had met to eat together, to hold hands and make plans, and maybe to part.

But Elvi's training as a nurse held her back from panicky flight. A nurse never ran, she behaved with sense and moderation, and took heed before she leapt to unfounded conclusions.

There had to be a simple explanation for everything. Lots of men had names beginning with R. Lots of men lived in Rome, and if Nicolina had returned from Rome with a baby and cases full of dresses with exclusive labels on them, it didn't mean that Rodari Fortunato had given her the child and the clothes.

A year ago Rodari had been seeing someone else, a woman worldly and lovely. He could not have found the time or the inclination to court Nicolina at the same time.

But remember, whispered the small voice of doubt in Elvi's mind, it was then the woman he loved had left him to marry another man. Hurt, disillusioned, needing to dull the ache in his heart, he might have met the runaway girl in Rome. A pretty thing whom he had noticed on his trips to the *isola*, who had not hesitated to accept his attentions and his gifts.

The girl had said of the other woman that she was lovely as a *contessa* camellia. Such a description would come easily from a writer, but a girl like Nicolina would not think of it alone.

"Oh . . ." Elvi cried out as a warm pair of hands closed with a possessive hardness on her shoulders. She was swung about and pulled into a pair of arms.

"You have been neglecting me, *cara,* and I am here to complain."

Trained not to panic, but driven quietly crazy by her thoughts, Elvi struggled against the embrace she would have welcomed an hour ago. Now Rodari's touch made her go cold. The sun shone above them, but a cloud of suspicion had darkened the day for her.

"I-I'm tired," she said. "Please let go of me."

He did so, abruptly, and stared down at her tense, white face. "The last few days have been a worry for you. They have spoiled our honeymoon ... such a pity, because I have just received a wire from Rome asking me to return so I can consult with the producer of *Bitter Grapes*. We leave tomorrow."

She gazed up at him, silent and despairing. If only she dared to ask if Nico was his child! If only she loved him less, then it would be easy to say the words.

"Then we had better return to the villa and pack," she said, and felt a profound relief that they were leaving soon.

"Delfina will pack for us, and I have booked an early flight from the mainland airport."

She nodded, and then saw curiosity glint in his eyes as he looked down at her. "We have had a good time here, and we can complete our honeymoon in Rome. I shall not be all that busy, but this new film is important to me and I wish to be on hand. Elvi, you knew our home would be in Rome ... the island is attractive, but it holds certain memories for me that are like shadows in the sun. I brought you here because I felt you would adapt more easily to my ways in surroundings not too worldly. Now you know me, and in Rome you will look and feel more relaxed with me."

"You mean, Rodari, that I shan't make a fool of myself and blush when people look at the pair of us and wonder why on earth you married a shy and unsophisticated mouse."

"My dear child," his smile held a mixture of mockery and ownership, "you aren't a mouse. By the time you have been dressed by a fashion designer and had a hairstyle arranged for you, you will be stunning enough in your own elusive way. I shall not be pitied by my friends."

"If you wish to change me to suit them ... oh, why did you marry me?" The words broke from her ... if only he had left her alone, left her to go on quietly with her nursing instead of pursuing her because her unworldly ways could not remind him of the woman he had really wished to marry!

"Surely you must know by now why I married you," he drawled.

"No, Rodari."

He quirked an eyebrow and teased the colour into her pale cheeks. "We met by chance and from the beginning there was something elusive about you that I wanted to capture. You were unlike other girls I had met and known."

"That sounds like a cliché, and you are too good a writer to deal in those."

His face became in a moment a bronze mask. "You are probing for a truth that may hurt."

"Try me, Rodari. I may prove braver than you think." She met his eyes and felt inwardly torn by a mixture of feelings. Was it a weakness, or a strength, to know that nothing on earth could kill the love she felt for this man who in every way was so foreign to her own nature? The shades and heat of Italy were in his very bones. He demanded love from her and gave his love to someone else. Perhaps her grey eyes revealed that she knew this; with a sudden careless shrug he made his reply:

"There is an old oriental saying, my dear. *It's better to light a candle than to curse the darkness.*"

She had asked for the truth and she accepted it. He carried a burning torch for someone else; she could only light a candle ... but in the darkness, and his heart had been dark during those days at the alpine inn, a soft small light could lead a person home. He had wanted to be led home, but now he was restless to leave the island for

Rome . . . and Elvi knew the painful reason. He had said they would stay for two months, now suddenly the honeymoon was ended and he was taking her away from the *isola*; hurrying her away with suspicious speed.

He flung an arm about her waist and walked her away purposely from the café on the cliffs. She didn't look back, but knew Nicolina was watching them as they went out of sight along the clifftop. It was later than Elvi had thought and the sun was beginning to set in a smoulder of softly violent colours. The air had grown sultry and the water of the lake had a metallic sheen, molten and still and holding the colours of the sky. In the stillness came the sound of chapel bells . . . sweet and sad, invoking a penance of those who had sinned.

Rodari paused on the hilltop and they gazed together at the sunset and listened to the bells. She strove not to look at him, and yet she did. The red sky seemed to light little fires in his eyes, and his features were as distinct as if carved. Her heart missed a beat, for how could she stay with him if he had betrayed Nicolina? How could she leave him when even yet he might be totally without blame in the matter?

"From the look of that sky we are in for some rain . . . a storm, perhaps."

A storm would be appropriate tonight . . . and it was as she dressed for their last dinner at the villa that lightning flickered across her room and seemed to rake the surface of her mirror. She gave a start and looked like a ghost in her pale chiffon dress with a sash of silver. She lifted her arms to clasp the pearl rosary about her neck . . . almost lost like Melisande's ring in the bottomless lake, but found among the rocks. Would she find again her lost trust in Rodari; her bruised faith and hope?

Again the lightning flickered and she heard the patter of rain on the foliage that draped her balcony wall. The sultriness had given way to a chilliness, or was it her coldness at heart that made her shiver? She took from the case already packed by Delfina the silky stole with the heavy fringes which, before her marriage, she had bought to wear on her evening off at the holiday hotel. She wrapped it around her so the fringes hung silky against the slight curve of her bosom. The rosary glinted through, a reminder always of her first morning at the villa. The sun had shone like a blade across the big double bed, and she had woken to find herself alone . . . the abandoned bride of a man who liked to swim in the haunted lake of his boyhood. When she heard him open the door she had closed her eyes quickly, pretending to be still asleep. She had heard him cross the room, and had felt his hands water-cool on her neck, and for a wild moment she had realised how easily a man could kill a woman. Silently, fooled by her closed eyes, he had fastened the rosary, still a little damp from the shore and with grains of sand clinging to it, and left the touch of his hand upon her tumbled hair.

What had been his thoughts that morning? Had he, in the burning sunlight, compared her to a woman far more lovely? And wished with regret that she could share with him the seclusion and beauty of the villa?

Immersed in her thoughts, Elvi found herself at the foot of the curving stairs, facing the Venetian mirror that almost filled a panel of wall. It seemed to draw her towards it, and to hold her reflection from her silver heels to her brown-gold hair, brushed away from her temples and held in the grip of a silver pin. Her hairstyle and the slender drape of her dress had a Grecian look, and so wide and dark-grey were her eyes that she gazed at herself as if at a stranger, and she saw that the stranger was elusively attractive.

Then a shadow loomed behind her and it was Rodari dressed in dark evening wear with a narrow silk tie against the white ruffled shirt-front.

For a long moment they were together in the mirror, but when she turned to face him they were apart.

"You look rather lovely," he said. "But *che triste*. Are you sad that tonight is our last night at the villa?"

"It is an appealing place," she said, unable to tell him why she couldn't smile tonight.

"And soon it will no longer be ours. Today I made a decision about the Villa Fortunato. For a long time the islanders have needed a rest home, a place where the elderly can stay and be cared for. My grandmother never comes here and Elena keeps busy in Rome with her social work since her young husband was killed. From tomorrow the villa will no longer be ours. I have arranged for it to be handed over to the local authority, and cash will be provided to run it and pay the staff."

"Rodari ..." For the first time in hours she felt like putting her arms around him and kissing the lean dark cheek. "What a very kind thing to do!"

"Call it a wedding gift to the young nurse I married."

"That's very gracious of you." She spoke huskily and felt the sting of tears in her eyes. Whatever his true motive in disposing of the villa, he made of it a gallant and memorable gesture. An old gold wine was brought up in cobwebs from the cellar and poured into lovely old goblets from the days of the Medici. They ate roast quail, and fresh peaches from the garden, and the lightning was shut out by the long velvet curtains.

"Strange there should be a storm tonight." Rodari wandered about the room with a goblet in his hand, a tall figure in his dark suit, restless and lithe as a prowling cat. Elvi had curled down slim and still in a winged chair, the ruby at her breast gleaming to match the ruby on her left hand. She listened to the thunder prowling over the turrets of the villa, and avoided her husband's eyes whenever they settled on her. She studied the soft glow of the lamps, or the deeper glow of the logs in the

55

fireplace. She was as keenly aware of their aloneness as on their wedding night.

"There is a superstition in our family that whenever trouble is lurking for a member of it a storm comes along." Rodari lounged against the black Italian marble of the mantelpiece and his eyes were almost as dark as the marble. "I have felt all day a sense of misgiving and this evening it seems almost a living shadow . . . hovering between us. I begin to wish I had not brought you to the *isola*. We could have found somewhere else to be alone."

"Why do you hate the *isola*?" Her lips asked the question before she could stop it.

He stared at her before answering. "There are always faces and places which fascinate and hold us against our will . . . just as I hold you, *carina*."

Her eyes grew wide with the shock of his awareness, and she watched as his lips moved in a smile that was neither tender nor cruel. It was indefinable, as he was, and in that moment there came a harsh clap of thunder that seemed to shake the roof. The storm was all around them and they were alone . . . yet so much stood between them, unexplained things, such as a heartless note to a fleeting love, such as the unforgotten love in his heart for that woman like a camellia.

Abruptly he set aside his wine glass and threw the last of his cigar into the fire. "I think we will get an early night, my dear."

He said it deliberately and her eyes flashed over his face that could still make her pulses race despite the secrets hidden there. She took in rapidly the black brows above the deepset eyes, and the Roman nose above the hard curve of his lips.

"Go on up," he said. "I shall put the guard in front of the fire and turn out the lights."

She left him without a word and ran all the way up the staircase with the scrolled iron balustrade; halfway up her stole slipped from her shoulders and fell to the stairs. She left it there and ran on until she reached the bedroom. She slammed the door behind her and stared at the key in the scrolled lock. She didn't want him to touch her tonight! She couldn't endure him after reading that note in Nicolina's bedroom. Her hand moved of its own accord and it was both simple and fearful turning the key in the lock, and then speeding to the dressing-room door to turn that key so he was doubly locked out. There was a divan in there, and he could sleep alone and not be consoled tonight by the wife he didn't love.

Elvi moved like a ghost to the bridal bed, as Delfina was fond of calling it. The carved bed with the madonna blue hangings and coverlet.

"I could cry a storm," she whispered to herself, and as the lightning raked the room she saw the door handle turn slowly to the left, then to the right. Then it ceased to turn and in the stillness that followed the thunder she heard her husband laugh. If he had broken down the door and slapped her for her defiance she couldn't have been more shocked.

He was not in love with her, so he could turn away from her bedroom door with a shrug and a laugh. That was what she thought until with a frightening suddenness the doors of her balcony were thrust open and she saw Rodari framed by the lightning. His black hair glistened with rain and his face was a hard mask.

"You don't know this house as well as I," he drawled. "There is room below with a magnolia tree outside the window that grows right up to your balcony. I may no longer be a Romeo, but I can still swing an active leg when I feel inclined."

"I -I don't want you here," she gasped, afraid of him and in a temper at the same time. "Can't you leave me alone?"

"If you had asked me, *cara*. If you had said you felt

57

tired after your duties as nurse to Nicolina, but you deliberately locked me out, and that I won't tolerate."

"I-I won't tolerate you!"

His face darkened and in a stride he reached her and seized hold of her. He gripped her hair and pulled just hard enough to force her head back against his arm. "Why did you run away from me?" His dark eyes raked her face and she flinched as a cold raindrop fell from his black hair to her cheek. "What did I do to make you behave like that?"

"I . . . I wanted to be by myself . . ."

"On this our last night together on the *isola*?" A smile that was not gentle twisted his lip, but at the same time it was not entirely cruel. "Is that why you are vexed, because I broke the news that we are returning to Rome in the morning? You think I am putting my work before my wife?"

"I . . . I'm just rather tired." She moved her head and her cheek was suddenly against his heart, beating strongly there beneath the material of his shirt. His wife . . . his possession. His to kiss as he began to kiss her, while outside in the night the storm passed on its way and the rain ceased falling on the lime trees and the magnolias.

"Sweet fool," he whispered. "Are you now feeling a little less vexed with me? Or are you vexed with yourself for not bolting the balcony doors?"

He left a kiss within the hollow of her throat, then swung her up into his arms as if she weighed no more than a little cat, and moved soundlessly across the deep carpet to the canopied bed. His eyes were magnetising in the lamplight . . . she was lost in his eyes, helpless in his arms, alone with the smouldering fires she could not control. Her hand felt weighted when she lifted it and tried to press him away from her. "Rodari, don't . . . please . . ."

"Make up your mind, *carina*." His fingers traced the veins in her pale neck and dwelt lightly on the soft curve of breast. "You are behaving like a vestal virgin guarding the sacred flame! By now, my vestal, you would have been entombed alive for having a lover and your hair would have been shorn off and hung from a lotus tree!"

He gazed down amusedly into her big grey eyes fringed by lashes so much darker than her hair. "Is my treatment of you so terrible?"

She gazed up at him helplessly, and then when he leaned away from her to loosen his tie she slid quickly off the bed and made blindly for the door, forgetting in her panic that she had locked it herself. He was laughing as she swung round . . . laughing wickedly as he swung her off her feet and tossed her to the bed without a trace of gentleness this time. . . .

. . . When at last she fell asleep she dreamed, and it was a dream bordering on a nightmare of a toppling cliff and a girl shrieking a name she could not catch . . . a dream that made her restless, almost feverish.

"Hush, be still, be still." Hands smoothed the tumbled hair from her hot temples and her pillow was turned on its cool side. The sudden coolness was delicious . . . like kindness after a blow. A tear stole down her cheek and stung the lips that had been taken . . . she had offered not a kiss, a caress, or a whisper.

Tonight, their last night on the island, she had felt despair and none of the rapture.

CHAPTER IV

For most of the journey by jet plane and then by cab from the airport Elvi sat silent, taking in everything with large eyes, and aware all the time that life in Rome would be new and strange to her.

Would she ever really know the man she had married? And would she fit into his sophisticated life and manage to forget that on the Isola Fortunato they had left behind them a mystery she didn't dare to mention? She could only wait and hope that he might one day speak of it and either justify her suspicion or render it harmless.

In the meantime they came to Rome the eternal city, with the Tiber flowing through it. old and knowing and reflective. Roof tiles and narrow streets were mellowed by the sun, and houses of the Renaissance lolled in shabby finery beside blocks of modern flats. Old palaces rambled around courtyards where children played and shouted beneath lines of washing. Motor-scooters and small cars dashed back and forth and despite the noise of modern living an aura of drama and romance lingered. The sunlight flashed on the great dome of St. Peter's and a flock of birds spun around it as if magnetised.

Rome of the seven hills, with its gaiety and piety and its full-blooded Latin love.

They left behind them the bustle of central Rome and the tempo quietened as they came to a more residential area. The sun played over the lion-gold of an old *palazzo* in a cypress garden, and they halted in front of the arched doorway. Shadow and sun crossed swords at the entrance and petals fluttered down from a flowering tree. History lay deep in the stone, and when Elvi stepped from the cab she realised that the *palazzo* stood upon a hilltop and that below lay the gold and green of the Roman arena. Bronze slates shone in the sun as it licked across the rooftops of Rome.

Rodari came to her side and she felt his fingers enclose her elbow. *"Roma, non basta una vita,"* he murmured. "Rome, a lifetime is not enough."

She gave him a slight smile and masked her nervous tension with an air of composure. They entered the *palazzo* in which his apartment was situated and went up to it in an iron caged lift. He had the rooms of the entire upper floor, and each room, he explained, had been modernised.

The door to the apartment was opened by his manservant Amilcare, a dapper little man with a waxed moustache and kind eyes.

"Welcome, *signora*. Welcome *signore*." He held wide the door and took swiftly from Rodari's hands the suitcases and the fur coat which Elvi had found too warm to wear on the journey. She stood a slender and uncertain figure in her cream linen dress with an Italian cameo on the shoulder. She wished she could have entered her new home with a smile of cool assurance, but she entered with a nervous look around her, like a mouse being enticed into a velvet trap.

One look and she knew that Rodari's cultured mind had chosen each item of furniture for this room, the *salottino*. There was a silvery grey sheen to the furniture with its sleek lines, and the long drapes were a blend of blues shifting together in the clear Roman light. Clusters of crystal lamps were fitted to the walls, and underfoot lay a carpet of deep blue. On a glass table top a stone dragon twined its tail and fixed the gaze with jewelled eyes. On a bookcase a porcelain cat stretched its neck and seemed to hold all wisdom in its slanting gaze.

Elvi wished pensively that it was a real cat curled warm and purring in one of the deep chairs, and she gave a start when Rodari gripped her shoulders and demanded to know what she thought of her new home.

"It's very lovely, and very smart ... may I look at the view from the balcony?"

"You may do anything," his fingers pressed against the fine bones of her shoulders, "but wait for the view when dusk falls."

"You say I may, but you hold me so that I can't."

"Because Rome is like an ageing beauty who is at her best in diamonds and mink. She is no longer a young girl who can step from her morning bath and look ravishing. I love Rome, and I want you to see her in soft lights and eyeshadow. She is like Venice and Florence, there are lines in her face, but her bone-structure is ageless."

"One could never speak of London like that."

"No, because London is all angles, but Rome is all curves."

"Do Italian men never stop thinking of women?"

"When they are asleep, perhaps."

She laughed with a breathless catch in her voice. "Rodari, how many women have you known?" It was the closest she had come to asking, the first time she had dared. She braced herself for the pain he could inflict with his strong, lean hands, but they slid with fire in their tips to her waist and then released her.

"No man reaches my age without a few affairs. Forget them, and remember only that I married you."

She caught her breath at his cool arrogance. "But why?"

"You keep asking me that and I shall be tempted to demonstrate the reason here and now, before we drink our coffee. *Grazie,* Amilcare. Yes, put the tray just there and the *signora* will wait on me."

He grinned as he spoke and Elvi quickly pulled off her wrist-length gloves and fought shy of his eyes. "Thank you, Amilcare. Those cakes look delectable."

He gave her a little bow and withdrew, closing the door with a Latin softness and suggestiveness. They were not long married. They would wish to be alone.

They sat down to their coffee, and Elvi slipped her feet as unobtrusively as possible out of her high-heeled shoes. They were smart to match her dress, but she was more at home in the casual type of shoe of her nursing profession. She felt the flick of Rodari's eyes over her legs and ankles, and she was again assailed by the half-frightened shyness of being desirable to this dark, strong Roman who lounged beside her and enjoyed the coffee she had poured out for him. There definitely lingered in this man she had dared to marry the arrogance of old Rome, when the young conquerors had taken it as their right to enslave a woman. She had read her history. She knew that very often a girl taken by a centurion would end by loving him ... it was a feminine weakness, the instinct to respond, no matter what, to the man who conquered.

"What I wonder do you expect of me?" He lit his after-coffee cheroot and studied her through the smoke. "A knightly being searching for the rose and the Grail?"

"I'm not that unrealistic." She bit the almond off the tip of a chocolate cake "I married a Roman and I know it now. After these days with you, Rodari, I am aware of life as never before. I feel the flowers growing."

"That is a very profound remark for a very young-looking bride." His eyes held hers in a long, deliberate, searching look. "I used to wonder what it would be like to possess another human being so totally that only I would exist for her. Nothing else beyond me would be of importance to her. Not her looks, her clothes, her home, or

63

even the child she might have."

"You're a Roman throwback," she threw at him.

"I think I must be. When the legions marched centuries ago to Britain I saw you there. You stood in the ripe corn and your hair was the same colour, and I made you belong to me."

"Meaning I could never have escaped from you, that what happened long ago had to happen again? That even if I had run away from the hotel you would have come after me?"

"Yes. No doubt you ran from me through the waist-high corn, but I caught you."

She gave a little shiver, for in her blood there had always stalked the awareness that in some other life she had seen his face before, felt his touch before, and was doomed to love him. Her lashes quivered and shielded her eyes as much as possible from his gaze that was so dominating. She was a woman and couldn't help but respond to that dominance, but all the same she craved a little tenderness and not just his pleasure in her youth and her fairness of skin and hair. These he found delight in as he would a peach plucked from a tree. He could, with equal casualness, discard her when the hunger abated.

"Ah, it feels good to be home again in Rome." He stretched his long legs and let his gaze roam the long cool room. Smoke drifted lazily from his lips, and Elvi tensed as his fingers crept from her wrist to her arm and up to the curve of her neck. With easy strength he drew her down to him and she caught the glint of fire behind his lowered lashes. Suddenly his shoulders were blotting out the room and the little cry in her throat was lost beneath the pressure of his smoky lips. Instinctively she struggled not to surrender to him, her slim body whipping back and forth among the silk cushions, trying to evade the kisses that pressed against her throat, her nape, her shoulders. They were too cruelly sweet and piercing. They melted her bones and made her heart ache.

"Y-you pagan devil!"

He laughed against her throat. "Because I kiss you, Elvi?"

"Y-you treat me like your slave."

"I treat you like a woman. Be happy that I do. Some men marry and then lose interest."

"Y-you don't care for me as a person."

"What nonsense. I like your kindness and integrity, they are so British. I like the way you listen to music with your fair head aslant and your grey eyes full of dreams. I like the smallness of your ears."

"Don't . . . oh, Rodari, don't!"

"You will really cry one day, *mia,* when I no longer kiss your ears."

With adroit strength he lifted her and carried her from the *salottino* along a corridor to the bedroom that would be hers. He held her with ease as he opened the door and took her inside. With a quirk of his eyebrow he dropped her on the bed. "I am going out for an hour," he said. "Make yourself at home, and remember that it is your home and you can do in it whatever you please. You can play music, dance barefoot, and eat *pasta.*"

"Rodari," she brushed the tumbled hair from her eyes, "may I know what time you'll be home?"

"In time for dinner." His fingers moved to his tie and straightened it. "I promised Lanciani I would see him today and we will be talking business. Get acquainted with the other occupants of the *palazzo.* A delightfully mad Baronesa lives on the lower floor, and we have also a ballet dancer who danced long ago in the Russia of the Czars. You will meet them in the gardens, and I promise you will like them."

"When shall I meet your family?" she asked.

He stared down at her and suddenly his eyes were

hard. "Elena will pay us a visit very soon, but I wish your meeting with the Contessa to be a little more formal. She will no doubt arrange a dinner party and we will be invited."

"It sounds terribly formal. Can't you just take me to see her?"

"I could, I suppose, if she and I were on better terms. But I rarely do a thing that pleases her. You, my pet, will please her less than anything I have done. So it is better you meet her when there are other people around and she must put up a front."

"Rodari, you're frightening me."

"Yes, where you are concerned I seem very good at it. Well, I never pretended that I or my family was easy to know. We are proud, arrogant and feudal, and you must consider it a blessing that unlike Sabinetta you are not forced to live under the same roof with my grandmother."

Elvi gave an uncontrollable shiver. "She sounds so formidable. Do I have to meet her?"

"Yes." He stood a moment looking down at Elvi, and as always his height and his arrogant grace made her feel strangely helpless and naïve. She wasn't a prisoner. She could refuse to meet the woman who had made his mother so unhappy, yet as her eyes dwelt on the obdurate moulding of his chin she felt defenceless. He had married her out of defiance, and he meant to enjoy his grandmother's indignation when he presented his bride.

His bride who was the opposite to everything she had hoped for him. Slight and fair; untitled and unworldly. A young nurse who had little to give him beside her love.

He bent over her and tilted her chin. He smiled quizzically. "I might not be a shining knight, *mia cara,* but I shall be there to protect you from the dragon. She knows she can frighten everyone but me."

"I can't imagine anything frightening you." Elvi took

in every detail of the face that was saved from being too handsome by the Roman nose and the dent in the base of his chin. These features intensified the character of his face and she strove not to believe that he was a seducer. Her heart turned slowly over, as it always must when she looked at him, and suddenly of their own accord her hands found his face and she offered her lips to him. He seemed to smile as he kissed her.

"You are a strange child, Elvi. Unaware of the small charming ways that made me want you. I don't deserve you, *mia,* but all the same I insist on the right to have you."

"Lucifer's bride?" She murmured the words almost unaware, and then flinched with pain as his hands gripped her and then released her.

"Yes. When people meet you they will no doubt think it. I should be back by the *prima sera. Arrivederci, angelina.*"

He left her alone, closing the door with firmness behind him, as if he imprisoned her in the bedroom with its pale golden furniture and its silvery drapes. She lay as he had left her and fingered the ruby ring that seemed to hold the Fortunato fire and fascination. Bride of Lucifer. It could be true in many ways, and only the future would prove how true.

She arose and went to the dressing-table and found that Amilcare had unpacked her case and laid out her brushes and comb and the little jewelled pots Rodari had given her, and the musical box she had bought in the Alps. She lifted the lid and the mountain tune drifted out as she combed her hair. Those first few days of knowing Rodari would always hold a magic that the music box would bring alive again. There in the mountains for a while she had thought him more wonderful than anyone.

She twirled her hair into a neat pony-tail and changed her dress for a more summery one in which the colours of

67

sea-green, pewter and pine mingled in cool harmony. The dress was sleeveless and she noticed a slight bruise on her upper arm and trembled again. What would happen if one day she felt driven to ask him the truth about Nicolina? Like most strong men he didn't always realise that his touch was painful. In a temper he might be capable of anything.

She turned away from her slim reflection in the glass and made a tour of her bedroom and adjoining bathroom. Everything was softly shining and up to date, and then to her delight she found herself in a little round boudoir with a deep glassed balcony and ivory wicker furniture set among trailing green plants. She didn't go to the balcony rail at first, but swooped on a small volume that lay on a table in the shade of the plants. She picked it up and found it slim and bound with deep red leather. She opened it and found it was a book of Italian poetry, and with little quick beats of her heart she took a look at the flyleaf to see if a name was written there. It was, beneath an engraving of two golden birds flying shoulder to shoulder, the symbol of great lovers.

"Camilla." Elvi spoke the name, and a sudden breeze seemed to whisper through the garden below. So beautiful, like a haunting perfume, like pale camellia petals in the dusk. Camilla, the name of the woman Rodari had loved. She had been here, as she had been to the island, and she left behind the kind of momento another woman would be bound to see. Elvi closed the book quickly, like someone who has looked into a forbidden room, and she replaced it on the table in exactly the position she had found it. There was no doubt in her mind that Rodari often read the poetry and looked at the golden birds who had flown apart.

She gave a little sigh and looked around for some means of escape from the balcony. She saw a narrow flight of iron-wrought stairs twisting down to the garden and careless of broken ankles she skimmed down them and found herself in a garden court of old tiles and cobbles and a rain-basin of stone with a spill of scarlet flowers around its brim. She glanced upwards and saw a wall around the garden, and corner towers that gave the place a secluded, watched-over look. She thought herself alone until suddenly she noticed an odd little figure poking about the bushes with a stick.

."That bird! That bird!" the person muttered to herself. "One of these days I will brain him!"

"Can I help?" Elvi approached out of curiosity, for the tiny woman was dressed most oddly in a long cloak fastened by a chain and upon her head she wore a sable hat that had seen far better days. She turned at once to look at Elvi and she seemed as frail as ivory, except for the lively look of wisdom in her ebony eyes. White hair peeped from the sable hat, and she had an odd, enchanting air about her that appealed at once to Elvi's imagination.

"I keep a raven for company, my child, and the wretched fellow will fly off with my few remaining treasures. He opens the box with his beak and is particularly enamoured of my pendant and chain. I have been searching for it and it will be a disaster if I can't find it. A disaster of the heart, you understand."

The little woman spoke in English, but it was slightly quaint, as she was, with an accent that wasn't Italian. She gazed at Elvi in a rather stricken way, like a raven herself in her dark cloak on a summer's day.

"I'll help you to look for your pendant," Elvi said at once. "Had you thought that he might have flown into a tree with it?"

"That wicked bird is capable of anything!"

"That magnolia tree with all those twisting branches looks a perfect hiding place." Elvi grinned. "When I was a schoolgirl living near Wandsworth Common I used to

69

love climbing trees."

The tree lent itself to a climber with its branches that bent and twined in all directions, and quite soon Elvi was lost among the cup-flowers and searching the nooks and crannies of the tree for the pendant. Suddenly there was a flutter close by and when she turned her head to look she saw the flick of dark wings and the glint of something jewelled in the grip of the bird's beak. She made a quick movement towards the raven, and startled by her, he let go of the pendant and it fell through the branches to the ground.

"I have it, dear child!" Its owner swooped on the jewel with a birdlike cry, and Elvi smiled down through the flowers. She looked and felt a child again, when life had been happy and carefree until the sudden death of her mother and the changes in the home which had followed not long afterwards. She had wanted to be friends with her stepmother and had tried to fall in placidly with her wishes and her new arrangements. But there had been no spark of affinity between them. Elvi had loved her own mother too much, and in the end she had left home to become a nurse.

She had never regretted her decision and had been a good nurse, until Rodari had come along to change her life of routine into a strange and bewildering sort of heaven.

She slid down a branch and landed lightly beside the small cloaked figure who was holding the pendant to her ivory cheek. The mixture of jewels were bright against the soft but furrowed skin.

"If I lost the pendant it would be like losing my life. It is all I have to remind me of the days when I was a young and attractive girl and so agile that I could leap halfway across a stage and land on the points of my toes."

"You are the ballet dancer," Elvi said, a note of enchantment in her voice. "My husband told me about you.

He said you danced in Imperial Russia."

"Yes ... so many years ago." The little woman glanced around and sat herself down on a low stone wall. She patted the side of it for Elvi to join her, and holding the pendant closely against her heart she studied the new and youthful resident at the *palazzo*.

"So you have a husband. Dare I ask his name?"

"I am married to the Signore Fortunato."

"And are you ravishingly happy, *matushka*?"

"Of course." Elvi flushed a little, for there seemed to be a very wise and knowing light in the ebony eyes that studied her so frankly.

"We used to say of happiness when I was a girl that it was a gift of the gods, like the gift to dance or sing. To some it comes. To others it takes the shape of mere contentment. Most sensible girls would wish for contentment, and no sensible girl would ever marry a man such as Rodari Fortunato."

"Don't you like him?" Elvi looked shocked, as if no woman young or old could possibly resist the man with whom she had walked to the altar of a Roman church, there to take vows in a language not her own.

"Of course I like him. To women of my age such men are terribly kind. But to a girl of your age such a man can be a charming but unpredictable devil. I know because I went through it as a girl. Look, I will show you."

The thin ivory hands shook a little as they opened the old-fashioned pendant set with a mosaic of jewels. Inside there was a miniature icon on one side and on the other a picture of a young man with bold handsome features and eyes with a faintly oriental slant to them.

"He was a Russian prince and an officer in the Imperial Army. I was but a poor girl who danced in the ballet at the Maryinsky. He loved me, and I worshipped him, but we could not marry. We planned to run away together to a country where it would not matter that he had royal

71

blood, but the revolution struck and Igor was killed when the peasants overran his father's estate and Igor tried to defend his mother and his sisters. I fled from Russia, for it was known that I had been his sweetheart. I took with me this pendant which he had given me, and though many times I have pawned it to pay for a room and a meal, I have never parted with it. The woman who parts with her lover's gift is a woman without a soul, and I had nothing else to put in its place. No child that would have looked like him. No other man who was so maddening and so joy-giving at the same time."

"You never loved again?" Elvi asked gently.

"I never loved again, or had lovers, not after Igor. There are some men ... they go out of a room and it is like salt forgotten at the table, or wine forgotten at a wedding. My hand in the hand of another would have been a thing of ice. My kisses would have been frozen things. As I said, my child. No sensible girl loves a man who is too much a man. She makes do with someone nice and ordinary."

"But look at what she misses." Elvi spoke almost unaware, and then blushed vividly at her own words. The little old dancer laughed and shut the pendant that held all her memories. "The English are usually clever at concealing their emotions, but you are obviously much in love with Rodari Fortunato."

"I – I suppose it seems strange to you that he should marry someone like me?"

"No ... and you must call me Lidija. I danced in the ballet, but I was never a great beauty. It isn't always true, you know, that very attractive men desire only beautiful women. My Igor had the pick of the women, and I never gave it a thought or a hope that he had noticed me until one night I came from the theatre into the chilly snow and he was waiting for me with a sable coat to wrap around me. He said I was so little I made him feel like a

72

giant and he carried me to his *troika,* which is a snow sledge drawn by a horse, and we drove through the snowy streets of St. Petersburg to the jingle of the harness bell. It was magical, like a dream without ending. Snowflakes lay like pearls on the fur coat. It was mine, he told me. I was to keep it. But I was shy in those days and I argued that the other girls in the ballet would think I was a good-time girl. How Igor laughed! He threw back his head in its fur cap and he laughed so loud that the quiet, snow-bound streets seemed to ring with his laughter."

Lidija paused, smiling to herself as she looked at Elvi. "Such an arrogant, self-willed man I found him. So untamed and passionate. He was a prince and he could have whatever he wished . . . except a ballet girl as a bride. But that night I knew only happiness. The frost had touched everything with a wand of silver, and he took me to a famous restaurant and we ate a midnight supper of caviare sandwiches and vodka in tiny gold glasses. Soon he was calling me *douchka,* his little darling, and I could not resist his wicked charm. But I should have resisted him, because ours was a happiness fated not to last. Already the revolution was flaring all over the country and everyone whispered of what would happen to those with royal blood in their veins. I loved Igor desperately and in the ballet I mingled with people who sprang from the peasantry and were ambitious to take the place of those born to rule. I knew that Igor was on the list of those to be killed. I pleaded with him to leave Russia while he still had his vigour and his life, and at last we made plans to leave together."

Lidija sighed. "Ah, it is all past history and I must sound tedious to a young girl newly married."

"No." Elvi reached out and touched Lidija's hand; it felt so fragile and made the girl so aware of all the years this woman had spent alone, having loved too much to ever love again. It was wonderful in a way, and yet it was

also sad. A grand love could bring a great happiness ...
while it lasted. Too often it ended in loneliness.

"It will be nice having you here at the *palazzo,* if you
really don't mind an old woman indulging her memories in your company." The ebony eyes that must long
ago have sparkled like gems in a face so piquant it had
caught the attention of a prince now dwelt intently on
Elvi's face. It was also a face without the symmetry of
beauty, yet it compelled the eye, held a certain enchantment that she seemed not to be aware of.

"You are still wondering how it came to happen, eh?
That you are married to a dangerously attractive man
who has seen life. Well, my child, it is now too late for
you to be sensible, or to have regrets. Accept that your
husband is a man out of the ordinary. Accept the tempest
and the tears, for neither can be avoided when a woman
chooses to love a handsome devil. Such men have their
abode between heaven and hell and they give of each to
the woman they choose to love."

Elvi lowered her eyes, for she could not be sure, as Lidija had been sure, of Rodari's love. She wondered if the
old dancer had ever seen Camilla in the *palazzo,* but she
couldn't bring herself to ask. She couldn't let people
know how very unsure she was of the dark and dashing
Roman who had taken her as his wife. Lidija was a gentle, sensitive woman, but there would be others who
would not be so kind, and she had to learn how to act. "I
suppose I feel a bit conscience-stricken really. A nurse
becomes so used to being always on duty, now I have more
freedom and I don't quite know how to cope with it.
Right now Rodari is out on business."

"And the good Amilcare takes care of the apartment,
eh? Relax, *matuchka.* Enjoy yourself being the pet of a
busy and successful man. Regard how such a man needs
you. Not to cook for him, or to sew on buttons, but to
help him unwind at the end of his busy day. You need

74

feel no guilt about that."

"To you, Lidija, I must seem very prosaic. Not at all the sort of woman for Rodari's sort of man." Elvi smiled wistfully. "I try to be what he wants, but I know there have been other more exciting women in his life."

"Are you jealous of them? It would be understandable. I was often crazy with jealousy when I came face to face with the other women Igor had known. It is perfectly natural."

Elvi thought of the woman she had not yet come face to face with, and her heart quickened anxiously at the prospect. It would be bound to happen. Here in Rome, at a party or in a restaurant, they would see Camilla and she would have to bear the agony of his longing for the other woman. She would have to look at the face that had a camellia beauty. She would see the dark silky hair that would be arranged in a classical style to suit the perfect face. The lips of Camilla would be dark red, and her smile would be like that of the Mona Lisa. Elvi knew her already. Beside that tall and lissom creature she would look uncertain and naïve, for Camilla had been made for a man like Rodari. She had been born to wear rubies; to grace his name and his home, and face without a qualm his social and business life.

"So you were a nurse, eh? And did Rodari see you in your uniform?"

"Yes." Elvi gave a slight smile and remembered the flick of dark eyes over the blue and white of her uniform and the narrowing of the eyelids as that dark gaze became more deliberate and dwelt on the little fob-watch that was pinned just above her left breast. That was the first time she had blushed all over. Being a nurse she knew that many things were possible, *but to blush all over*.

"It must," she said quickly, "have been exciting in the old days to dance in the ballet.'

"Yes, it was." The many tiny lines in Lidija's face

75

broke into a smile and then came together again in gravity. "The dancers were always on their mettle on the nights when the royal boxes were occupied. They used to try and outshine each other and the rivalry among us was very intense. Sometimes after a display of my own I would hear someone laughing softly in the darkness of the theatre. It amused Igor when I showed off my ability to hold an arabesque longer than the other dancers. He would say afterwards at supper that if I danced like a duck he would still love me. I would keep begging him to tell me why he chose me for his girl when others at the Maryinsky were so much prettier. And do you know what he told me? He said that I had no one else in all the world to love but him, which meant that I gave him all the love I had to give. Yes, it was an arrogant point of view, but what girl could resist a man who commanded that she belong entirely to him? He would not even allow me to keep a domestic pet. He gave me a young stallion and made me learn how to ride him. Once when I had a fall from the stage he carried me to the sauna baths and he made me stay there until I ached no more. He could be cruel, but I would have died with him."

Lidija gazed at the pendant which long ago her prince had fastened about her young neck. "He could take me everywhere but to his home, and he was there on the day the peasants rose up and attacked the age-old system of master and slave The old Prince, his father, had not been a harsh master, but when the rebellion came the kindnesses were forgotten and only the injustice of being a bondsman was remembered. I heard afterwards that Igor died holding in his arms the body of his young sister Natalia. In many ways I have often envied Natalia."

"Don't say that," Elvi begged. "For many years you were a dancer and you gave pleasure to a lot of people."

"Yes, I used to dance for men and women, now I write stories for children. Your husband – and don't jump,

76

child, when I use that word – was good enough to introduce me to a publisher and now I make enough to supplement my small pension so I can live out my days in this old and romantic *palazzo* in Rome. I hope you will like living here. We overlook the city and in the evenings the view is magical."

"Rodari forbade me to look at the view until the *prima sera*."

"And have you disobeyed him and looked?"

"No – oh, it isn't that I want to be slavishly obedient to his wishes, but I want to see Rome as the dusk falls."

"To make a memory, eh?"

"Perhaps." Elvi reached out and cupped a nearby blossom in her hand; a lemon flower that reminded her vividly of the *isola*. "One can never be wholly sure of the future. What is real today can be a dream tomorrow."

"You are afraid of the future."

"Yes, a little. I've not yet met any of Rodari's associates and friends, and I may not fit into his life. He is an unusual man, the sort of man I never expected to meet, let alone to marry. I – I feel somehow inadequate."

"I wonder if he thinks so?" Lidija smiled and patted Elvi's cheek. "You have nice skin and big grey eyes, *matuchka*. You are slender and shy, and untouched by anyone but the big, dark, and so distinguished Fortunato. He may think himself a fortunate man to have a cool-looking bride with the warm heart of the English. Don't you know how much we emotional and intolerant foreigners admire the British?"

"Is it enough for a wife?" Elvi asked. "To be admired for being cool and tolerant?"

"You speak as if you doubt your husband's love."

"I – I can't help myself."

"Because for a while there was someone else?"

"Because I think he married me to have his revenge on Camilla."

"Ah, you know her name!"

"I saw it written in a book, in our apartment. I'm sure she's as beautiful . . . in fact as gorgeous as her name."

"Yes, she is very beautiful."

A little shudder ran through Elvi; not one of envy but of resignation. "I know she married another man."

"The marriage was a celebrated one and much publicized. It isn't every day that a beautiful young *contessa* marries an American oil millionaire."

Elvi looked amazed. "But I was told she was betrothed to this other man as a young girl."

"Quite so. He went to America to make his fortune and there he took out American papers and became a citizen of that country. When he became rich he returned to Italy to make Camilla his wife. There was a rumour that he had an illness that could not be cured. She married him, and now he has been cured by a new remarkable drug. They are a wealthy couple. The facts of their life get into the newspapers and that is how I know about them."

"Everyone must know," Elvi said quietly. "It must be common knowledge among Rodari's friends . . . and I have to face them. I have to put on a brave show . . . the English nurse whom he married at random, as a gesture of defiance, I – I shall be pitied, and perhaps scorned, and at this moment I almost hate him. He had no right to marry me!"

"Would you have felt better if he had made love to you without making you his wife?"

"I wouldn't have let him make love to me!"

"No, *matuchka*?" Lidija gave a gently mocking laugh. "Such men have the gift of seduction, and if Rodari Fortunato had wished to seduce you he would have done so before you could catch your breath to deny him. Girls are not like men when it comes to love. They are the vulnerable victims of their love, and clever men like your

78

husband know this. He could have made you his with or without a gold ring."

"And I must be grateful that he married me?"

"If you love him."

"I – I don't know any more." Elvi jumped to her feet and gazed at the *palazzo* in a defensive way. Suddenly with its corner towers and its grilled balconies it seemed like a prison. "I keep coming up against his past life . . ."

"Did you expect an angel?"

"No, not the dark angel. He calls me Lucifer's bride himself."

"His little joke, surely?"

"Not entirely. Oh, why didn't he leave me alone to go on with my nursing? I was content. I didn't ask to live in a Roman *palazzo* with an impossibly attractive man."

"Many girls would like to be in your shoes."

"I had an interesting career."

"So did I, child, and I would have suffered two broken legs to have in its place the man I loved. What man is perfect? Especially a man in his middle thirties with the face of a Roman god."

"His face isn't that perfect."

"Quite so." Lidija gave a laugh. "Now stop being foolish and flaunt that ruby ring he has given you. Let him dress you in nice clothes, and let him kiss you all night if he has a desire to do so. He's a man. Rejoice in that, and forgive him for being also a bit of a devil. Think of all the exciting things you would have missed if you had married a prosaic young doctor with duty always on his mind."

Elvi looked at Lidija and a small grave smile clung around her lips. "I'm glad I have a friend living at the *palazzo*."

"My dear child, call on me whenever you wish. My rooms are on the ground floor, and a young raven for company is not the same as a young girl with whom I can be nostalgic about the old romantic days. Many thanks for finding my pendant. Without it I should feel very lost."

Elvi felt the sting of quick tears and blinked them away. How ungrateful she was! She had Rodari, for better or worse, and in her heart she didn't wish again for the loneliness of being a shy young nurse in a strange country. Soon he would be home again. He would stride into the *salottino,* bringing with him that look of vigour and splendour that made it impossible not to love him ... not to forgive him for being rather more of a devil than Lidija realised.

"I had better be getting back to the apartment. I've loved talking to you, Madame Lidija."

"And I have enjoyed meeting you, *matuchka.* Always it was a pleasure to dance in England. Once upon a time a very charming Englishman wished to marry me, but it would not have been fair to become his wife with longing in my heart and body for my dearest Igor." Lidija looked frail and sad as she sat in her dark cloak on the mossy wall, while the sun slowly turned red-gold in the sky over Rome. The birds twittered more noisily in the trees, and once again that cool breeze stirred through the garden.

"*Do svidania, matuchka.* Till we meet again."

CHAPTER V

THE lights of Rome were like scintillating moths of the night beyond the balcony of the *salottino*. Elvi waited no longer to look at them. The darkness had long since fallen, but Rodari had not returned for dinner. Elvi had sat down alone to eat the delicious meal which Amilcare had cooked for two people.

Now, her wine glass in her hand, slender in her white dress sashed with silver, she stepped out on to the balcony and made alone her memory of Rome at night. Magnoias were trained over the balcony ironwork and the blooms fitted into the palm of her free hand; cups of cream with a sweet scent. A little storm of feeling shook her heart. On this their first night home he might have put her before his business friends . . . if indeed he was with Lanciani, the producer of the films based on the Fortunato novels.

How still was the night . . . how lonely for her, way up here above the city that was so alive with people and lights. Couples would be sitting outside the cafés and on the terraces of the restaurants and music would be playing. Dark eyes would meet and smile, and hands would come together on the table tops.

Elvi sipped her wine, but it didn't soothe the ache in her throat. Rodari had promised to be home by duskfall, but now it was past nine o'clock and Amilcare had cleared the table and put out the candle flames and said discreetly that he would keep the *signore*'s dinner over a flame in case he had not dined. Of course he had dined. Careless of his promise to her, he had chosen the company of his friends . . . or another woman.

The suspicion stung sharply and she drew away physically from the creamy flowers that made her think of a cream-skinned face and night-dark hair framing lovely cheekbones and gemmed earlobes. Was it possible that Rodari was with Camilla? Driven to seek her out on his return to Rome; unable to stay away from her despite his marriage to someone else? A marriage still young enough to be called a honeymoon!

"*Signora?*"

She spun about and saw Amilcare standing in the opening of the balcony doors. He wore his outdoor coat and carried his bowler hat in his hand.

"Will the *signora* be all right if I leave now?" he asked.

"Of course, Amilcare." She knew he had an elderly mother who disliked being left on her own at night. "Dinner was very nice and I enjoyed it."

"*Grazie*. I have left coffee for the *signora,* and will now say goodnight."

"Goodnight, and give my regards to your mother."

"The *signora* is kind." He gazed at the slim, white-clad figure who seemed to shine softly in the reflection of the starlight. He gave her a little bow and withdrew and a minute or two later Elvi heard the front door close behind him. She was alone in Rome, with only her thoughts for company, and the moths that flitted ghost-like among the magnolias.

Tormented thoughts are not good company, and she sat alone on the balcony with them, until a church clock chimed on one of the hills and she realised that it was eleven o'clock. She went indoors and turned out the little burner upon which Rodari's dinner had been keeping warm. He wouldn't want it ... no more than he had wanted her company on this her first night in Rome.

She went to her room and prepared for bed. Somewhere in the *palazzo* someone was playing a radio or a record. It was an aria from an opera of Puccini and it suited Elvi's mood as she sat at the dressing table and brushed her hair, the silk sleeves of her robe falling back from the pale slenderness of her arms. The soft burning lamp beside the bed gave the room a blue mood, and Elvi had decided already that tonight she would sleep here alone. She would feign sleep when Rodari came home ... if tonight he came home.

Her hair hung straight and fine to her shoulders when she stood up and turned away from the mirror. She despised the look in her own eyes. It was too unhappy, and she wanted to be untouched by whatever Rodari did to hurt her.

She wandered about the bedroom, over the soft carpet of silver-grey. The small boudoir chairs were of blue silk, and on a little table stood a vase of dark-red night roses. The bed was an unusual swan shape, and a great cloud of chiffon draped it. It stood upon a dais with steps leading up to it. The sheets were of fine silk and the counterpane was of silvery brocade. The room in the balletic shadows of the single lamp was perfectly lovely. The long mirrored doors of the dress closets opened without a sound to reveal Elvi's modest wardrobe.

"We will fill that from wall to wall," Rodari had said. "As my wife you will be expected to look chic. I want you to have all the things you never had before."

Silk dresses and heartache, she thought bitterly. Lace lingerie and a lonely apartment while he meets Camilla.

The drifting music died away, and somewhere in the apartment a shutter creaked. She could smell the roses, dark-red and velvety like the lips of a woman. Restless and pent up, she took a book and curled down on the *chaise-longue* to read it. The little Venetian clock chimed on the bedside table, and she tucked her feet beneath the hem of her robe and looked small, like a child, her soft hair half-hiding her pensive profile. When the clock struck again she would go to bed, but first she would finish this chapter and try to understand Rodari through his novel. This edition of *The Princess Caprice* was in English. It's fascination was complete and she was lost again in him, a rebel and at the same time a victim. She felt in total sympathy with Caprice when she cried out to the man in her life: "I hate you for hurting me and I wish I could run away from you, but I'd be leaving my heart behind for you to go on breaking."

Elvi glanced up slowly from the book. Yes, it would be like that. No matter how fast she ran, or how far she went, she would never escape from him because like a fool she had given him her heart to play with or break. He played with her heart tonight and did it so carelessly. If he returned he would not find her sitting up for him. She concealed his book behind one of the silverwork cushions and went over to the bed. She slipped out of her robe and climbed into the swan bed and felt the coolness of the silk against her bare arms In the darkness the roses gave off a stronger scent, and Elvi buried her face in the big silk pillow and prayed for sleep. If she fell asleep she wouldn't know if he returned or not. If she slept he wouldn't wake her.

She was drifting off when the sound of a key grated in the lock of the front door and brought her sharply awake. She half sat up, then lay down quickly again. Her heart was racing. Her every nerve was on the alert. Temper ran alive through her as she heard Rodari whistling to himself as he entered the *salottino*. He paused to switch on the light. A moment later a spoon clinked against a cup and she knew he was pouring himself a coffee from the steel pot that kept the heat for several hours. The aroma of a cheroot stole through the rooms, and once again a spoon clinked against china. Soon he would finish his coffee and his smoke. Soon he would open her bedroom door and the light would stream in from the corridor. He would approach the bed and lean over her to see if she lay waiting for him.

She closed her eyes tightly. He would not have the satisfaction of finding her awake. He would find instead a wife who appeared not to care whether he came home or stayed away.

She tensed, the awareness of his coming thrilled through her. The door opened abruptly and the light from outside speared the darkness so that even through her closed lids she sensed him standing tall and inquisitive in the doorway.

He moved within that ray of light, making no sound on the thick carpet as he came to her bedside. He leaned down to her and she felt his breath on her hair ... and there was wine on his breath which the cheroot smoke could not conceal.

It was the shock of it that altered the rhythm of her breathing, and at once he sensed that alteration. "I know you aren't asleep," he murmured. "When you sleep you lie as still as a little lizard in the sun. Right now you are trembling."

"I am not!" She threw off his hand and rolled out of his reach to the other side of the bed. Instantly he snapped on the lamp and they glared at each other in the blue-shaded glow of it.

"You've been drinking," she accused him in a frigid voice.

"Yes, a glass of two of champagne to celebrate a victory over Lanciani. He wanted a certain actress friend of his to play the leading role in *Bitter Grapes*, but I talked him out of it. I wanted Rosa Angelica or no one. No film. No big gross at the box office. No *Lion d'Or-*

award for my director-producer friend to add to his collection."

"So once again you got your own way."

"Yes, *mia cara*." His eyes narrowed as he stared down at her, for her expressive young face couldn't hide the hurt and the anger of being left so alone all the evening, tormented by the thought of where he was and with whom. Even yet as she looked at him and saw the ruffled black hair and the slumbering fires in his eyes she felt that swift stab of uncertainty. He was too wickedly attractive to be held by a young, naïve person like herself, too experienced and worldly not to have plausible excuses on the tip of his tongue.

Her hands clenched the silk coverlet and she felt in herself the desire to hit back, to hurt him in return. "I suppose like a timid little bride I must believe that it took you all this time to get your own way. It usually takes you less than an hour."

"Are you doubting my word?"

"It's past midnight, and you did promise to be home in time for dinner."

"My dear girl, I hope you aren't trying to domesticate me."

"I just hoped that you might keep your promise."

"I have never made out that I am the ideal husband who comes in on the dot of six and spends the evening with a pipe and the paper. I am involved with the kind of people to whom midnight is the hour when they start to enjoy themselves."

"Midnight for me was the watching hour."

"Here in Rome it is the witching hour. I came home, in fact, with the intention of plucking you out of your nightdress into a dance frock. I thought we might go and dance for an hour or two at the Café Casanova."

"Was I suddenly on your conscience?"

"No, *cara*. When I talk business I rarely give anything

else a thought."

"Doesn't Signor Lanciani have a wife to go home to?"

"He's a divorced man."

"I thought divorce was disliked by Italians."

"His wife was an English actress. It was she who obtained the divorce."

"I see." Elvi's fingernails bit deep into the silk upon which she was curled in a tight defensive ball. "Is that why you married an English girl?"

There was an intense silence in which the soft ticking of the clock seemed to grow louder by the minute. Rodari stared at her and his face assumed that look of a bronze mask with only his eyes alive and glittering. Then his body came alive and he began to move round the bed until his tallness was right there beside her and his darkness against the soft gold of the drapes was a blow to her senses. She felt the tautening of her body, the quickening of her heart, the traitorous, undeniable, silent crying out for the love he denied her. It was unthinkable that she could love anyone so arrogant, and yet with every bone and breath she loved him.

"I never cherished the illusion that you married me because you couldn't do without me. I – I must have been blinded by your glamour, but now my eyes are wide open."

"Wide and so grey," he said, in a soft and dangerous voice. "Big and lonely and not far from tears. Tell me, *cara*, what a monster of thoughtlessness I am. Throw that pillow at me if it will help. But don't accuse without justification. Do not insinuate without the scent of another woman on my jacket. It was wine, not perfume you caught on me."

"Will it be perfume next time?"

"It might if you don't take warning and stop this!"

"Must I never speak my mind? Is that a privilege reserved for the Italian husband?"

87

"It's a privilege reserved for adults, and you are being a bit of a brat tonight."

"It's gallant, I suppose, for a husband to make promises he doesn't intend to keep?"

"Were you so disappointed that I wasn't here to share with you your first *prima sera* in Rome? Well, allow me to make up for my absence." Swiftly he bent over her and before she could fight him off he swept her up into his arms and was striding with her to the balcony doors. They were partly open to let in the air and he thrust them apart with his foot and carried Elvi outside in her filmy nightdress. He carried her right to the edge of the iron parapet and held her poised above the city, where the lights of the nightclubs still shone brightly.

"Rodari, this is mad!" She clutched his shoulders in alarm and felt the hard muscles and the warmth of him right through the silk that like her lingerie had been spun and sewn by the nuns of an Italian convent. Suddenly he bent his head and his eyes laughed silently into hers, and then his mouth touched her throat and travelled to her breast and it was pagan beyond belief to be kissed in this way high above the city of Rome.

The balcony rocked and Rodari dragged his lips from her soft skin. The lights below seemed to dip and sway, and then with a soft oath Rodari was dashing inside with her. He made across the bedroom to the corridor and they had reached the stone archway across the passage when once again the earth shook and somewhere in the street tiles clattered to the pavement.

"The *terremoto*," Rodari muttered. "A summer quake that will throw a few tiles and break a few windows ... if we are lucky."

Elvi clung to him while shutters banged and people hastened down the *palazzo* steps to the cellars that long ago had been dungeons. Rodari didn't suggest they go down. He held her with a bruising closeness and when everything was utterly still again he took her back to bed and tucked the covers around her. "*Buon riposa, amica.* The earth won't shake again."

She gazed up at him and suddenly their quarrel seemed to hurt more deeply in this moment than before the earth tremor. "Rodari . . ."

"Elvi?"

"I'm sorry I behaved like a child. It's just that I felt so very much on my own, but I do realise that business must come first."

"I wonder what business you thought I had? A clandestine meeting at a *pied-à-terre* outside the city with another woman?" A slightly cynical smile raked across his face, and he drew a finger down her cheek. "You must not be so uncertain of your own charms. Such soft skin, like a peach . . . am I forgiven, then, for leaving you on your own?"

"Yes . . . people should never part without making up a quarrel."

"Are we about to part?" He quirked an eyebrow, a black peak against the Italian darkness of his skin.

"Y-you said goodnight to me." She gazed into the eyes that held a slumbrous fire, and there rippled through her the confusion of loving him after being so angry with him.

"That, *amica,* was five minutes ago." His dark eyes roved her face and dwelt on the slim arms and slender neck in the blue lamplight. His arms slipped around her and he drew her to him, not protectively as before, but possessively. His lips found hers and she had to cling to him as once again the earth shook though the *terremoto* had passed away.

Elvi knew that before long she would be plunged into her husband's social life, so she didn't demur when Rodari suggested that she go with him to a Roman fashion house to buy clothes for all occasions.

They drove there in his car, through the thick, fast traffic of Rome, past the steeples and domes and rather gaudy blocks of flats. Elve was fascinated by the ancient jostling elbows with the modern in this city of the infamous Colosseum, where they paused to take a look at the decaying splendour of it. There they walked beneath the ramparts where long ago the lions and the Romans had roared while the martyrs died.

She gave a little shiver and felt Rodari's lean fingers grip her elbow. "It must have been quite a spectacle, eh?"

"Pagan," she murmured, and her eyes flicked his profile etched against the blue sky; the imperious nose, the mouth that was firm and yet full-moulded, the cheekbones that told of generations of breeding, and the eyes with their deep-set, lash-deep setting. On a wall nearby an old woman sat selling cherries, and with an impetuous movement Rodari went to her and bought a brimming basket of the dark red fruit. They ate them walking back to the car, and as they were driving away he shot her an indulgent smile.

"The cherry juice is all round your lips," he said. "Adalia Domani will think I have married a child."

He drove the Lancia along a smart boulevard with trees shading the shop fronts and they parked on a little green and walked across to the Romani Fashion House, aloof behind gilded doors and oceans of deep carpeting and long mirrors that reflected the curving desk where a young receptionist gave Rodari a flustered look and grabbed at the telephone.

"*Si, signora,* I will send them up right away." Colour stung her cheeks as she showed them to a gilded lift, which swept them up to a splendid showroom where the chandeliers were like great jewels hung with smaller jewels, and the stucco walls were rampant with nymphs and urchins and sea-horses. It was like a ballroom, and Elvi backed away from the wicked glint in her husband's eyes.

He laughed and studied her. "Do I still make you shy?" he mocked.

"You make shy every woman you look at." To avoid his eyes Elvi took out her compact and quickly renewed her pink lipstick. She was sure the girl at the desk downstairs had thought they had been kissing!

"This seems to be a very expensive place," she said nervously.

"One of the most expensive, *mia cara*. You should feel flattered that I want you to have the most beautiful clothes in the whole of Rome."

"Fine feathers for Jenny Wren?"

He took a step towards her, and then paused as someone approached them across the shell-pink marble floor. It was a tall, dark, swan-graceful woman who wore a long green velvet skirt and a cream satin shirt cut after the style of a man's. "*Amico mio,*" she held out a hand to Rodari, "how nice to see you again. I heard you were back in Rome, and as always the city seems more Roman when you are here. You had a pleasant vacation?"

"Extremely so." He raised the woman's elegant hand and kissed the back of it. "I found for myself an English bride ... did the grapevine pass on to you that intriguing piece of information?"

"I heard a rumour, but ..." The woman turned her dark head and stared frankly at Elvi. "Yes, English without a doubt, and you want me to dress her?"

"From top to toe, Adalia. From her ears to her ankles, and for every occasion."

"My dear child," Adalia Domani held out her hand to Elvi, "let me welcome you to Rome, and as the bride of Fortunato you are indeed welcome."

"Thank you, *signora*." Elvi felt the cluster of rings bite into her hand, a brisk, friendly bite that she liked. The high priestess of Roman fashion was a forthright woman, but her eyes held humour and a hint of Latin *simpatica*.

"So, Rodari, you have at last surrendered to the challenge of marriage. There will be long faces in Rome this summer. You were always the bachelor who aroused the keenest interest in the wealthy matrons with daughters to dispose of in the marriage mart."

"Don't pretend to be cynical, Adalia." He gave a laugh. "Everyone knows that you enjoy dressing brides more than you enjoy the races."

"You give me complete freedom to dress your bride?"

"I give you *carte blanche*."

"And no supervision, *amico mio*? I may send you about your business for the next few hours?"

"I have every intention of leaving Elvi in your capable and charming hands. You will find her an amenable child, and if you run a pin through your hand she will deal with it. She was a nurse when I found her, only don't dare to dress her so that she looks too neat and shining to be touched." He glanced at Elvi and deep in his eyes there was a look that was vitally intimate for a brief but intense moment. "Give me a surprise, Adalia, when I return at lunchtime to take her to meet my sister at the Apollo Gardens."

Elvi caught her breath. "You said nothing this morning about meeting Elena!"

"No." His eyes flicked her face with its look of alarmed surprise. "I had something else on my mind . . . but as a matter of fact she rang me early and suggested that we lunch with her. She is eager to meet her brand new sister-in-law."

"I expect she is curious, like everyone else."

He laughed and looked at Adalia. "My bride is worried that my friends will think I have married in haste only to repent at leisure. A fabulous wardrobe from the House of Domani should help her to have more confidence in herself. And now," he shot a glance at his wrist-watch, "I am off to the film studios. Lanciani and I disagree about everything at the start of a film, but somehow it sets the mood for an exciting production."

"The mutual antipathy of two highly talented men, eh? Who work at their best with daggers drawn." Adalia smiled at Elvi. "Clever men can be such children at times, and they can also be as subtle as the devil himself. My dear, how did you dare to marry this man?"

"With the aid of a minor avalanche I swept her off her feet." He took Adalia's right hand and kissed it, then bending over Elvi he left a kiss on her temple. "*Arrivederci*." He strode away, tall and dark against the pastel colours of the showroom, a masculine breeze through the scented air, a tiger purring of the lift and then silence.

"That man is a dynamo." Adalia gazed frankly at the girl he had married so swiftly and secretly. "And like a bit of silver you are caught and held by him. My dear, I don't know whether to envy you or to console you. Are you . . . happy with him?"

"Happiness is a simple word with many meanings," Elvi half-smiled.

"You love him . . . very much?"

"I love him . . . regardless."

"Regardless of the many rumours, eh?"

"He's far too attractive not to have been involved with women far more glamorous than I."

"Would you like to look glamorous for him?"

"I should like to look as nice as possible."

"Then come along with me and we will look at materials and decide what style of dress and costume will suit your cool English looks. It is to your advantage that you are so fair among Romans . . . I wonder if Rodari will kill me if I send you to the *salon* to have your hair restyled. A pageboy is nice but a trifle dated, and I would like to see a soft fringe above those eyes of yours. Hmmm,

I think your colours are silver, evening violet, and a touch of flame. The colours of courage and a hint of the puritan. Come, *cara*. When I have done with you I think you will please your Roman."

Within a short while Elvi was in her slip and surrounded by gorgeous lengths of silk, satin and chiffon, not to mention velvet and the softest tweed. Adalia and her male assistant swirled these stuffs around her and discussed her figure as if she were a mere doll who couldn't blush to have her bosom cupped in a pair of square, brown hands and likened – in Italian – to young roses.

"The waist is breakable." The hands slid down to enclose it. "The hips will take a thousand fine pleats in that chiffon velvet."

Elvi met the young designer's eyes and was deeply startled to find them wholly masculine in a most amused and unholy way. He knew the trend of her thoughts and he secretly laughed at her. He assisted Adalia in the design of lovely clothes for all types of women, but he wasn't in the least effeminate. He looked, in fact, rather cocksure and ugly, until she noticed the rough curly hair, the lopsided grin, and the almond-shape of his brown eyes.

Adalia addressed him as Raf. There was a certain raffishness about him, but there was also a curious, almost exciting gentleness in his touch.

"That violet-shadow cloak would suit the *signora*," he remarked. "You remember we made it for the ambassador's wife, but she thought it made her look too pale."

"Yes, Raf. Clever boy. Please fetch it and we will see how Elvi looks in it."

He strolled away, lean and active as a male dancer, with something of the panther in his tread. He returned carrying the garment over his arm and he came quite close to Elvi before swinging it around her and enclosing her in the fabulous folds of velvet the colour of an evening sky and trimmed from the collar to the hem with softest

94

fur. He drew the collar around her face and studied her with his almond eyes that gave him a look of the Orient, or certain parts of Russia. Elvi couldn't believe he was Italian; to her the bold, strong looks of her husband spoke of Italy, but this man had an appeal that was almost primitive, making her think of Borodin's music and wild ponies racing across the steppes.

"You look nice in the cloak, *signora*." He spoke politely, but his eyes said something that made her pull away from him.

"Rodari will like that garment," said Adalia. "You must have it, *cara,* and I think this silvery cloth will team well with it, a simple almost puritan style to set off the richness of the cloak. A perfect outfit for the opera."

"Or the ballet," Raf murmured. "A box above the stage and a single rose pinned to the cloak."

Adalia had turned aside to give instructions to a couple of her sewing girls, and Raf spoke these words so they were audible to Elvi alone.

"Stop it!" She spoke back in a whisper, alarmed by the way this man was flirting with her.

"Adalia, may I dress now?" She clutched the cloak around her slip-clad figure, suddenly and acutely aware of having been touched by Raf. Her husband would look murderous if he knew ... she saw vividly in her mind's eye a picture of Rodari swinging the back of his hand across the raffish face of the man who confronted her. It was almost shocking that such a man mingled with women in the intimacy of the dressmaking salon and learned their secrets.

"Yes, you patient child, we have finished making a model of you, and when you are dressed Raf will take you down to see our hair stylist. I should like you to come one day in the week – with permission from the new husband, of course – to have your hair restyled to suit the new clothes. In the meantime, *cara,* wear the little cherry suit

95

which doesn't need a stitch altered."

Elvi took it with her into a cubicle and after she had put it on she couldn't help but like the gay and perky air it gave her. Its simplicity she knew to be expensive, and she bit her lip as she gazed at her reflection in the cubicle mirror. She knew her husband to be highly paid, but whatever would she do with a dozen day dresses, half a dozen evening gowns, and sundry other articles for wearing at the beach and the golf course; on the café terrace, and at the theatre. It was exciting to be bought so many lovely things, not to mention shoes, handbags, gloves and costume jewellery, but would she ever wear them all?

She stepped out of the cubicle, almost into the arms of Raf Stefano. He laughed at her with his eyes and indicated that she precede him into the lift. He pressed the button and they swept downwards. "There are some women on whom first-class design and fabric are lost. If I may say so, Signora Elvi, you have the perfect body for the clothes I design. That suit is one of mine. I deliberately measured wrong the client for whom it was intended. I must have had a premonition that you would appear and like the glass slipper it would fit you."

"I must confess," she gave a laugh that held a faintly nervous note, "that I feel a little like Cinderella. All those clothes!"

"And a Prince Charming to go with them."

She shot him a look, detecting in his voice a note of irony. "I'm very grateful to my husband for his generosity."

"I think he is the one who should feel grateful. Lots of women have charm, but it's cultivated, especially in Roman society. He brings you to the capital like a rather lovely flower he has plucked at the wayside. I wonder if Rome is the place for you."

"I hope it is, *signore,* as I have come to live here."

The lift came to a halt and they stepped out. "We go

this way." His fingers brushed her arm in a subtle way. "Your husband bears an illustrious name, *signora*."

"Do you think that's why I married him?"

"You?" He gave a laugh that was also subtle. "You would have to love a man, or feel a need in him for your compassion. Whatever people will think when they see you with him, they will never mistake you for a gold-digger."

"What do you think, *signore*?"

"That like Rhea you strayed into the dark forest and met Mars."

"How ridiculous!"

"When people scoff at something it's because they can't face the truth. Here we are." He paused at the reception desk of the beauty salon and asked that an appointment be booked for the Signora Fortunato. "Make it for Thursday, around eleven o'clock."

When they were out in the foyer again Elvi gave him a look that was amused and also a little indignant. "Italian men are so bossy!"

"I am only partly Italian." He smiled and his almond eyes took an attractive slant that made him seem boyish and at the same time very wise in the ways of the world. "My mother came from Bavaria; an old, remote part of that country with some fascinating customs. She was more of a gipsy than anything else and I take after her in some of my ways. Do you think I look a gipsy?"

"Yes. I can imagine you with a ring in your ear." Then Elvi glanced away from him and assumed a look of coolness. He was too puckishly appealing to be friends with; too much the sort of young man who liked women and was liked by them. Rodari had told her to make friends in Rome, but Raf Stefano was not the sort of friend he had in mind.

"It must be about lunchtime," she said, making her voice cool. "My husband should arrive soon ... oh, talk of the devil!'"

Raf gave a low, meaning laugh as a tall figure came striding into the foyer, lean and forceful in smooth grey suiting, with an air about him that made other men seem awkward.

"I will leave you," Raf said, "and see you Thursday."

She wanted to say no ... she wanted to insist that there could be no hint of friendship between them, but the lift swallowed him just as Rodari reached her side. "*Buono,* you are all ready and waiting for me!"

"Yes." She gave him a smile and thought how splendid he looked in grey. "I'm longing to meet Elena."

"Excellent. I am sure Elena is eager to meet you ... she always insisted that I would never find anyone tolerant enough to stand my dictatorial ways."

His gaze as he spoke dwelt on the gilt-iron lift into which Raf had vanished like Puck.

"Who was the young man in the balletic trousers and tan shirt?"

"Adalia's assistant." Her heart gave a slight thump. "He designed this suit I'm wearing. Do you like it?"

Rodari deliberately looked her over. "Very much, *mia.* The colour and style are so right on you that I suspect him of having second sight. He must be new to the establishment. The last time I came here – it would have been about a year ago – Adalia had someone else working with her."

Elvi walked out into the Roman sunshine with her tall husband and allowed him to take her arm as they crossed the road to the parking green. His touch seemed to shoot exquisitely tiny arrows right through her bones, and she felt powerless to resist him even as her doubts about him came painfully to life again.

With whom did you come to the fashion house a year ago? the question clamoured. Was it with Camilla ... or that girl who returned to the Isola Fortunato with cases

98

of fashionable clothes?

He opened the door of the black Lancia and she slid inside. He shut the door and started the engine and everything was so outwardly normal, and so inwardly disturbed. "Put your hand in my pocket," he murmured. "I bought you something flippant to show off to my rather too earnest sister."

Elvi shrank from touching him and had to force her fingers to steal inside his jacket pocket for his gift. Her fingers came in contact with a little box and she took it out as gingerly as if it could burn her.

"Open it.' His tone was slightly impatient. "You won't find a snake inside."

She found a slim gold bracelet with a ruby heart charm attached, a trinket to delight her, and at the same time to impress upon his sister that he liked his bride well enough to give her such charming trifles.

"It's very pretty," she said, and her fingers shook a little as she clasped the bracelet about her wrist and felt the swing of the tiny heart. "Thank you, Rodari."

"The charm of you, my sweet," he drawled, "is that you remain so polite with me, so almost restrained, as if you had quite forgotten that last night I held you in my arms."

"And is the bracelet a sort of payment for that?"

There was a stunned silence, and when Elvi dared to glance at Rodari she saw that his jaw had set like rock and his entire set of features had about them a look of deep cold anger. "I wonder, *jeune fille naïve*, if you would dare to say a thing like that if we were not in a car in heavy traffic? Would you?"

"I hope I don't feel terrified of you."

"I sometimes wonder if you know what you feel for me." And as he spoke he turned the car in through the scrolled gates of the Apollo Gardens.

CHAPTER VI

THE drive curved around clusters of flowering trees and shrubs and they came in sight of the lawn where people were dining at tables shaded by colourful parasols. They parked beside the pavilion where musicians played and made their way to the terrace where Elena had said she would book a table for three.

Elvi breathed the flower-scented air and stroked the bougainvillea that clung to the trelliswork of the long terrace. She felt a little nervous about meeting her sister-in-law for the first time and wondered if she resembled Rodari.

"There is Elena!"

A young woman had risen from one of the tables and was waiting for them with a slightly diffident smile, as if she weren't quite sure of herself in this moment of meeting Rodari's wife. She must in the past have met some of the other women in her brother's romantic life, and Elvi knew with amused certainty that she would be surprised by the woman he had chosen to marry.

The surprise was there in her eyes, a flash almost of shock as Elena looked directly at Elvi for the first time. It was hardly flattering to come as a shock to someone, but Elvi tried not to mind as she was formally introduced to Elena Chiavari, who was attractive without being beautiful in a pale mauve linen dress worn with a picture hat of pale straw. Her eyes were lovely; the deep, lustrous eyes of a real Italian girl.

"I have so looked forward to this," she said. "I have wondered often about you, Elvi, and tried to picture you in my mind. The reality is so much nicer than the image I made up for myself."

"*Cielo,*" Rodari gave his sister his most diabolical smile, "do you actually approve my choice of a bride? No doubt you were warned by *la nonna* that I had probably married a film starlet."

"Don't let us argue today," Elena pleaded. "We shall never agree about *la nonna,* so it is best that we don't discuss her. Now shall we sit down and have a drink?"

"By all means." His smile in an instant became affectionate and he bent his tall head and kissed his sister's face beneath the wide brim of her hat. "You are looking attractive, Elena, but a trifle pale. I think it would be a good idea if you took Elvi around Rome and showed her the galleries and fountains and romantic old ruins. You could also go to Lazio and sunbathe. Why not?"

"I should enjoy it." Elena smiled across the table at Elvi. "You are new to Rome, of course?"

"Yes, a complete stranger, but a fascinated one. I'd love to visit St. Peter's."

"We will make a date to do so. I have my social work on Mondays and Wednesdays, and unless *la nonna* wishes me to go shopping or driving with her I am free to do whatever you wish." Elena shot a smile at her brother. "I expect Rodari is busy with the new film.'

"It would please me if you two made friends." He beckoned the white-coated waiter. "Would you both like Campari aperitifs before we look at the menu?"

"That would be nice."

"Perfect," said Elvi, and suddenly she felt more relaxed in the sun on the terrace and was glad that Elena was so different from the haughty beauty she had imagined. She was quiet, self-contained, and her mauve dress was an indication that she still mourned her young husband. Elvi glanced from the sister to the brother and thought how strikingly apparent it was that they belonged to the *aristocrazia* of Rome. She was glad Rodari had bought her the cherry-coloured suit; to look smart in his company was important, and it helped also to boost her morale.

"And what do you think of *bella Roma*?" Elena asked when their drinks arrived. "I know Rodari chose to live at the *palazzo* because of that magnificent view of the city."

"It is breathtaking," Elvi agreed, and felt her husband's dark glance pass over her profile. She suspected that he smiled a little, amused again by the way she had rounded on him for leaving her alone last night, ten thousand lights at her feet and a lonely balcony to share them with.

"Do you find as a stranger to Rome that you feel more alive than you did before? I know other cities are exciting, but Rome has a warmth of heart about it, an appeal to the senses . . . do you find this?"

Elvi gazed into her drink and felt that sense of awareness stir through her; she was learning what it was like to be married to a passionately alive man, and she was learning all this in the city of love, both sensuous and pious. Its domes and steeples a symbol of the love that was both earthy and heavenly. Everything conspired to play on the senses as the fountains played on the stones. Dark eyes seemed to hold more fire than the blue eyes of her own country.

She glanced up, straight into the dense eyes of her husband; they seemed amused by her seriousness as he handed her the menu. "Choose your own lunch," he said. "It will be good practice in reading Italian."

"Are you studying our language?" Elena asked. "From choice, or because Rodari is bullying you?"

"Tell Elena I don't bully you," he said. "She seems possessed of the idea that I must be a terrible husband. You may look this child over for bruises, Elena, but you won't find many."

Elvi grinned slightly as she recalled a bruise or two. Men! They didn't know when they were hurting a woman, either physically or mentally. They thought torture began with the rack. In reality it began with doubt ... the gnawing little doubt born of an initial and a baby boy with real Latin eyes.

She pulled away from his eyes and studied the menu. "I think I'll have devilled chicken and peppers," she said.

"An association of ideas?" Elena murmured.

"Perhaps." Elvi felt his leg move against hers and pretended she didn't feel it. "For a starter I fancy watermelon. Do you remember the one we ate on the road to the island ..." She broke off sharply. "No, on second thoughts I'll have minestrone."

"The melon would be cooler." Rodari's voice seemed to hold a cool note, as if her abrupt change of mind had reminded him of the island and its secret.

"I – I like minestrone."

"Then by all means have it." He shrugged and turned to Elena. "You look as if you live on sips of honey and good works, *amica*. How about a *pizza* heaped with anchovies and tomatoes? The sort old Maria used to give us on the island when we were children. She used to bring them to the house in her vegetable cart, remember, and the Contessa always swore that she was a witch."

"She could tell fortunes," Elena reminded him. "She told me when I was twelve that I would marry two men. She was wrong there, of course. I shall never marry again."

Rodari ran his eyes over the menu and then glanced up lazily. "Do you ever see anything of that American airline pilot who flies for Italia Airways? He rented that small villa on the estate outside Rome, did he not? And painted in his spare time."

"Primitives." Elena fingered her rings and her face was shadowed by the brim of her hat. "His Italian friends call him Guido, but his name is really Guy Stacey. Yes, he still lives at the villa and has parties there. He sends invitations up to the house, but I never go. What would be the point? I feel nothing any more for other men. I am a Fortunato and we only love once . . . it's in the blood."

"You will be lonely, Elena, if anything should happen to the Contessa. She is not getting younger and uses a stick now to get about."

"A pearl-handled one." Elena smiled slightly. "She insisted on that."

"She has always been insistent."

"Aren't you, Rodari? You really are more like her than I am . . . perhaps that is why you clash whenever you meet. It is better for two people to be opposite in temperament if they are to find harmony together. Anyone can see that Elvi is your total opposite."

"You think I married for harmony?" he drawled.

"Whatever your reason, *amico,* I am glad for you now I have met your wife." Elena looked across the table into Elvi's wide grey eyes. "I hope your family in England won't miss you too much, *cara.*"

"I have no family any more . . . that was the reason why I came to Italy to work. I felt that a little travel would broaden my mind."

"I think you must be extremely broad-minded," Elena smiled, "to marry a man like my brother." She cast him a look as he conferred with their waiter. "He can be maddening, but I will admit that he can also be charming. Italian men are the greatest charmers in the world, and they also sing well. Have you heard Rodari's baritone?"

"Only in the bath," Elvi smiled. "He seems very fond of *La Donna é Mobile.*"

"He must take you to the opera. The theatre season is ending, but wonderful outdoor performances are given at the Baths of Caracalla, under the night sky of Rome. Few things are more memorable. Rodari, we must take your wife to see and hear some real Italian opera."

"I intend to make her fond of all things Italian." He tasted with appreciation his *risotto* of mushrooms and saffron, and proceeded to talk about Puccini and Verdi, whose music he favoured for its richness and melody. It was as if it didn't suit him to become involved in a discussion about his marriage, and with assured ease he made their luncheon as light and gay as the sweet they ate at the end of it. An ice-cream bombe called a *cassata,* which had whipped cream and fruit encased in the ice-cream. It was delicious, and after they had coffee they took a stroll through the Apollo Gardens.

They were lovely, with grottoes and pools shaded by flowering vines. A cool avenue of giant cypress trees led to a small arching bridge of tawny stone, aged by time and velvety with lichens. They came to a leaf-hung Tuscan temple set among bushes of red camellias and peonies of pink and white with deep hearts.

Elvi took in the fusion of lovely colours and the thought came stealing that this was a place for lovers.

She gave a start when Rodari touched her arm. His fingers lay tanned and lean against the cherry-red of her suit . . . so light a touch, yet it flickered through her like lightning. It possessed her, reminded her that she was his, and she could feel herself rebelling against it. It wasn't enough . . . not nearly enough to be owned as if she were a Lenci doll; a toy to be dressed and taken out, if he felt inclined.

She pulled away and ran into the little temple. A spider had stretched its silken threads across the entrance and she brushed them away from her face and watched the spider go into hiding behind one of the wall frescoes. A shadow slanted. She swung round and saw Rodari towering in the doorway. There was no escape for her . . . no escape for him from the love he was compelled to give to someone else. Neither of them moved for several seconds, and then it was as if a stone Apollo came to life and pursued her into the temple.

His hands gripped her shoulders. "You are tantalizing me," he said. "I see fear in your eyes and I want to know why it's there. I give you things. I take you to meet people you will like. I try to be as good to you as I know how. What more do you want?"

"Please . . . let's go outside! Elena will be wondering . . ."

"I am wondering." He forced her to meet his eyes. "Are you deceptively sweet and cool and innocent? Do those grey eyes seem limpid to me because I can't always read them? Is it the name and the money you prefer to the man you married?"

"No!"

"No, *mia cara,* it can't be love. A woman in love doesn't shrink away from a touch, or go pale at a kiss. What a dilemma for you! Attached by Roman law to a man whose kisses you don't want. Did you fondly imagine that I meant to treat you like a daughter? I am not quite old enough for that, or as yet unmoved by the look of you. For each gift I expect my reward . . . that, my dear, is the way the game is played, whether you like the rules or not."

"You are the one who plays a game," she retorted, "and I don't like being your pawn."

"My pawn?"

"Yes, so you can pay back your grandmother . . . and that woman called Camilla: I've been told she's utterly beautiful, so I suppose you married me just to prove you weren't looking for a substitute."

"I have never liked substitutes," he agreed, his face like iron. "And in every way you are the direct contrast to Camilla. You are fair and she is dark. Shy where she is assured. Candid instead of subtle ... and she is a great beauty who has been painted and photographed by every famous artist. You wanted to hear me say all this, and now I hope you are satisfied."

"I am sorry, Rodari." She brushed past him into the sunshine again, where Elena stood admiring the scarlet camellias while she smoked a cigarette in a short holder. The smile she gave Elvi was thoughtful, and Elvi couldn't help but wonder if she had caught a little of that conversation in the temple.

"Camellias," she said, "always strike me as rather artificial."

They returned to the car and Rodari gave his sister a lift as far as the office where she conducted her social work. During the drive she arranged to meet Elvi the following day so they could take in some of the Roman art galleries and attend a small cocktail party some friends were giving.

"That will be all right with you, Dari?"

Elena used what must be a family nickname, and Elvi felt a small stab of envy. She would have loved to know Rodari before he had met and fallen in love with Camilla.

"Yes, fine with me. I don't want Elvi to be lonely at the *palazzo* while I am involved at the studios. It will be different when I start my new novel. I shall then be working at home."

"What is the new book to be about?"

"Men and women." A smile creased his lean cheek. "Their loves and their hates. Nothing is more fascinating than the manipulation of the emotions."

"I hope, Dari, that you confine your manipulations to

your fiction."

"Meaning?"

"You asked me about Guido Stacey. I believe you would like me to become involved with him . . . in a nice way, of course."

"You are young, Elena, and very attractive. You can't live with a dead lover."

"I doubt whether I could live with a man I did not love. What could be more terrible for a woman?"

"Loneliness . . . not having a shoulder to weep on, or someone to fight with. At this time you feel young and independent and able to cope, but what of the time ahead when you return to a empty house and only the polite greeting of your maid? I know you have your friends, but they have their husbands and lovers."

"You are old-fashioned, Dari. A Roman throwback to match your looks. The absolute male who believes that a woman is incomplete without a man. Perhaps she is, but women, unlike men, have to be in love to be able to find happiness. Without that flare of love there is no desire."

"Even for women, Elena, there can be desire without love. I speak as a man who knows."

"I look at you, Dari, and I am sure you have been allowed into every secret known to woman. All the same all women are not alike, and I don't wish to be coerced into a love affair or a marriage I might regret. I shall manage . . . and *la nonna* is too fond of life to leave me on my own just yet."

"Yes, she is tenacious of life. What a pity Sabinetta had to die so young and so lovely."

"Please, Dari. That is all in the past, and *la nonna* has regretted often her lack of understanding. Because of it she knows she has lost your affection . . . Dari, why not forget old wounds and be friends with her?"

"My dear girl, if the Contessa wished for that, would

she completely ignore the fact that I am back in Rome with a bride? She has not telephoned or sent a word of congratulation. A few flowers for Elvi would have been a nice gesture, but no, *la nonna* ignores us both – and you ask me to offer the olive branch."

"The pair of you have too much pride." Elena glanced at Elvi and her smile was one of fond exasperation. "Don't forget, *cara*, we will meet tomorrow by the Fontana dèl Tritone about two o'clock. I hope you like looking at painting and sculpture?"

"I want to see everything Roman."

"Until tomorrow then." Elena stepped from the car. "*Arrivederci.*"

"Goodbye . . . it was so nice meeting you."

Elvi turned to wave at the slender figure on the bustling pavement, and then the Lancia sped on and Rodari was silent for the remainder of their journey home. It seemed to Elvi that he was still angry about the confession she had forced from him in the little Tuscan temple. Camilla was all the things she could never be. Dark and lovely. Self-assured and full of subtlety. Men liked that. They enjoyed being teased and mystified . . . tricks that were not taught to busy young nurses, who saw more of pain than glamour.

When they reached home a large, beautifully wrapped wedding gift awaited them. Elvi looked eagerly for a card, and Rodari said drily that it was probably inside and the best way to find out the donor was to unwrap the package. He proffered the small silver knife from his pocket and watched with a kind of lazy alertness as Elvi cut the seals and ploughed through layers of wrapping paper until she reached the box. Sprawled across the lid was a famous Venetian name connected with glassware, and Elvi glanced at her husband before he could veil the flash of danger in his eyes.

"Open the box," he ordered.

"It has come from Venice." She spoke hesitantly, and felt how quickly her heart was beating.

"I can see that. Lift the lid and look at the contents."

She gazed at him a second longer, then she bent over the box and with hands that had lost their eagerness she lifted the lid. She parted the nest of damask-soft paper and her breath caught in her throat as she exposed a cut-glass gondola designed for displaying fruit, and at each side of it a crystal-stemmed goblet, each one perfect and shimmering. There was a tiny envelope enclosed, and her fingers shook as she took out the card . . . she knew the handwriting at once, though only once before had she seen it. Slender and elegant, wishing them a happy marriage, and signed not by a single lovely name but by the combined signatures of Signor Lucius di Montini and his wife the Contessa C. Silvanos di Montini.

How dared she! The words rang through Elvi's mind as she stared at the card. Camilla had sent the gift of crystal, a reminder to Rodari's bride that she had known him first; a subtle intrusion into their home, and their life together. Rare objects, to remind them both of her own rare beauty.

Elvi drew away from the gift as if it could bite, while Rodari lifted one of the goblets and seemed to caress it with a lean hand as if he caressed Camilla. "You must write a note of thanks," he said. "It was good of the Montinis to think of us."

"I am sure the Contessa has thought of nothing else!" Elvi swung on her heels and marched away from him to her bedroom. She half-feared that he would follow her and raise a storm, but he left her alone, and she took a shower in the cool green cubicle with brush paintings on the glass walls. She stood beneath the warm prick of the water and told herself mutinously that she would like to smash the wedding gift. It made her so mad that she must accept it. To refuse it, even if Rodari would let her, would make it unbearably plain that she was jealous of Camilla.

She turned on the cold water and caught her breath. Lovely, shimmering crystal to remind Rodari of things Elvi could only half guess at. Trips in a sleek Venetian gondola, perhaps. Their own wine in a basket complete with goblets on long stems. A moon and a tenor serenade as they floated along, held close in each other's arms.

The scene was all too vivid, and Elvi swished out of the shower cubicle and tied the sash of her robe with angry movements of her hands. Her hair hung straight and damp about her shoulders as she stepped out on to her balcony, a quiet hideaway with its wicker chairs and scarlet cushions. She strove not to look for the little red book, the one with the poems and the lovely name inside. The table was blank. Perhaps Amilcare had taken the book away, for he would know of the rapturous interlude his master had known with one of the great beauties of Roman society.

Elvi sat down in an easy chair shaped like a fan and rested her head against a cushion. She felt a desperate need to relax, to be calm and objective about her marriage. What a primitive gladness would have been hers if Rodari had said of the crystal: "It would be discourteous to return such a gift . . . we will give it away to charity."

Elvi closed her eyes and felt the late afternoon sunshine slanting scross her bare throat, a caressing warmth that made a drowsiness steal over her. Could anything be more emotionally disturbing than to be married to a man you adored and distrusted at the same time? Could anything be more bewildering than to be swept into close relationship with a man whose world was subtle and stylish; in which good manners in public took precedence over hurt feelings in private? She drifted into a doze, emotionally worn out, fair and slight in the scarlet-cushioned chair.

She awoke with a sudden shiver and realised that the sun had gone in. She uncurled out of the chair, stretched herself and went indoors. Everything was quiet and enwrapped in the final moments of the Roman siesta. She combed her hair and clipped it away from her face; applied soft pink colour to her lips and felt soothed by her own siesta. She decided to go and make a pot of coffee. Amilcare, thank goodness, wasn't the sort of manservant who begrudged her the kitchen. She was the *padroncina,* he had said. He would be only too happy to show her how to prepare the *padrone's* favourite dishes.

The kitchen was bright and modern, and it was pleasurable to smell the aroma of crushed coffee beans, to listen in the quietness to the purring of the percolator, to rest the eyes on the soft white and lemon decor.

Elvi placed the pottery cups on the tray and poured the hot and fragrant coffee into the matching pot. She found the cream, sugar and biscuits and carried the laden tray in the direction of the study. Her instinct told her that Rodari was there, working on his film script or making notes for the new book.

She paused to open the door and then noticed that it was already ajar. She was about to push it wide when the voice of her husband, and the words he spoke, made her go as still as a bird. He must be talking on the telephone and she heard him say plainly: "When on that impulse we flew to Venice you knew we would become lovers there. It was inevitable as the stars and the tide, and because we were lovers then we can't meet now as polite friends. You never miss the Charity Ball in June, so I will see you there, and I will know you no matter how elaborate the mask you wear. . . ."

Elvi stayed to hear no more. She fled back to the kitchen and stood for a long chilled moment staring at the wall. The tray grew heavy and she put it down on the table. So it was in Venice where her husband had made love to Camilla, and she had sent as a wedding gift a crystal gondola to remind him of their love in the city of drowned palaces, of bells across the water, and the confetti of a thousand pigeons ... the magic of the lagoon with the moon trapped in the jade green water.

Elvi swallowed drily and like an automaton she poured herself a cup of coffee. It eased the dryness of her throat, but still her nerves were as taut as a bowstring and she tensed as she caught the sound of approaching footsteps. A tall figure darkened the doorway and Rodari strolled into the kitchen. "Ah, *buona,* you have made coffee like a good girl, and I was longing for a cup. When I work I always get a thirst for coffee."

He lounged against the table while she poured his coffee and handed him the cup. She found herself unable to speak to him. There seemed no words, only the hurt and anger of being betrayed by him in the home he had told her was hers.

His eyes were upon her as he drank his coffee, their look was one of laziness on the edge of alertness, as if he shared with great cats that instinct for being relaxed and wary at the same time. There was in every line of his powerful body that grace of movement that made him so swift in attack, so lethal in his attractiveness.

His glance stole over her, taking in the rose silk robe that clung softly to her slim body, revealing in a subtle way its physical awakening, but also a tenseness, a withdrawal, a sense of outrage. He pretended he had been working when all the time he had been in long-distance conversation with the woman who would not let go of him ... the dark lover she reached for with greedy hands again, pretending they could only be friends, knowing all the time that to love Rodari was to feel anything but friendship.

The feeling of outrage quickened. How dared he look at her like that when his thoughts were full of that other woman whom he planned to see again at the Charity Ball, which was a highlight of the social scene in mid-June, a sort of masked revel just made for clandestine meetings.

He reached for a chocolate biscuit as if he had nothing but casual thoughts and a slight hunger to assuage. His white teeth crunched the biscuit and he slowly quirked a black eyebrow. "What a baffling young wife you can be," he drawled. "You make delectable coffee for me, but you don't say a word to me. Are we still at odds over the wedding gift? What would you have me do with it? Shall I drop it from the balcony and smash it into fragments on the cobbles below?"

"Would you do that?" she asked.

"As if Lucrezia Borgia had sent us poison cups?" He laughed lazily. "What a child you are in some ways, but because of that, and your nun-grey eyes, I forgive you."

"Thank you," she murmured, turning away from the smile on his lips. It wouldn't be quite so easy to forgive him, and impossible to forget that with childlike trust she had loved that dark and devastating face and thought it miraculous to be his wife. It was because he liked her innocence that he had married her. What would be his reaction if she told him that two could play at intrigue and if he meant to go on seeing Camilla she would not sit in a corner of his life like a little nun, wearing the rosary he had given her on their wedding night.

Today he had given her a ruby heart, and she glanced at it with quick pain in her eyes.

"Soon you will have a wardrobe of rubies," he murmured. "Next it must be earrings, tiny ones because you have such small ears."

"I shall think you have an uneasy conscience if you keep giving me gifts," she said, and her arm stole out of

114

sight behind her, hiding the bracelet which carried a heart of stone. It was to Camilla he had given his heart of blood and nerves. Her beauty, flawless as that of a white camellia, still held sway over his feelings, and Elvi felt powerless to compete with it. She could only rebel inwardly, and wonder if she would turn to ice when next he touched her, pulling her hard and close to him, pretending to himself that he held Camilla.

"You talk of my conscience," he said. "How am I to judge what is real about you, and what is false? I can only look in your eyes and see my own face reflected in those huge pupils." He took a step towards her, and she backed away from him. Her head was up, her chin was set, her body refused to yield. She stood at the other side of the table and clutched it like a shield. It was too soon after hearing him make his assignation with Camilla. Not as friends, he had said, but as lovers!

"You should ask yourself, Rodari, if you always tell me the truth!"

"Would you like that . . . the complete truth about myself?"

She stared into the glinting darkness of his eyes and her heart was a little hammer beating at her breast. No . . . with sudden panic she couldn't endure the blunt words spoken in this white and lemon room redolent of spices and grapefruit, the domestic things of married life. She would have nothing left, no faint hope at all, if in that deep and deliberate voice of his he described in detail what he felt for that beautiful creature other men had painted and photographed.

"I . . . I don't want to hear!" Her face had gone as white as the wall behind her; its contours were fine-etched and with her entire being she was aware that love was only real when you felt it to be unbearable.

"The one thing you could not endure would be a revelation of my feelings, eh?"

"Spare me that, at least." With a faint, brave shadow of a smile she began to wash the coffee cups. In a while Amilcare would want to prepare dinner and she didn't want the kitchen to be untidy for him. Though she was the mistress of this apartment she felt like a stranger in it. She wiped the cups and knew exactly the moment when Rodari turned and left the room, walking away with that long supple stride of his. She listened and heard the door of his study close behind him. It was a significant little sound . . . like being shut out of his heart.

CHAPTER VII

Elvi came out of the *salon* with a velvet cap perched at an angle on her glossy, fringed hairstyle. She looked stylish, and perky, as people do when they are troubled at heart but determined not to let other people know. She walked across the carpeted foyer to the imposing doors and was about to hail a green taxi-cab when someone came and stood behind her and spoke above her cherry-capped head.

"Would the *signora* accept a ride in a conveyance far more interesting than a fast noisy taxi-cab? I am sure the *signora* is not in a hurry to get home quickly to an empty apartment."

She spun about and was not unduly surprised to meet a pair of harlequin eyes set in a face with a quizzical sort of charm about it. "Raf . . . you!"

"At your service." He gestured across the road to where a horse-drawn cab stood waiting patiently. The horse had flowers tucked into its harness, and the driver wore a blue jacket. The old-fashioned conveyance looked festive and an irresistible smile touched Elvi's lips.

"I believe you were waiting about deliberately," she said.

"I confess it." He laughed, looking down into her wide eyes, so grey in contrast to the cherry cap, so dark-pupilled and softly lashed. Elvi didn't know it, but she took on an elusive beauty when a man looked into her grey eyes. Such English eyes in a city of bold dark looks. Her smile spread slowly to her eyes. Raf Stefano was so attractively raffish in a black and brown sporty jacket worn over narrow trousers with beneath the jacket a lemon-coloured sweater with a turtle neck. His hair was slightly disarrayed, black with brown tints as the sun touched it . . . unlike Rodari's which was raven in the sunlight. As her husband came to mind she panicked for a moment and felt she must hurry away from the temptation in Raf's slanting eyes. It was as if he knew of the flaw in her marriage, catching her like this, with the sun shining over Rome, offering her the fun of a ride in a horse-drawn cab.

"For all you know," she said, "I might be in a desperate hurry to get home."

"I hardly think so." His smile was boyish and a shade wicked. "Adalia received a call from the film studios this morning, asking her to design the clothes for the new production. It was your husband on the line . . . she called him Dari, which I believe is the term of affection used by those who have known him for some time."

"I may have his lunch to prepare."

"Is the perfect manservant on leave?"

"You really are an impudent person!"

"No, merely a man who would like to take you for a ride, and maybe at the end of it to give you luncheon. I mean well."

"You look a satyr to me, *signore*."

"I assure you that looks can be deceiving. You look a mere girl who is bewildered by the world, yet you are the bride of Rodari Fortunato."

"You say that as if Rodari would marry only a sophisticated woman."

"Those of Roman society know his taste in women. Is it any wonder there is speculation about his bride?"

"What are your speculations, *signore*? Have you

decided yet whether I am a noodle who fell by chance into a dish of truffles, or a little opportunist who used her nurse's wiles to lure a Roman plutocrat to the altar?"

He smiled rakishly and flicked his eyes over the cherry cap that perched upon her brown-gold, fringed hair. "You are like a calm day that might suddenly hold a storm ... we found that cap after you had left the shop the other day and I sent it to the *salon* this morning in the hope that you would wear it. It goes well with your dress."

"Thank you." She fell into step beside him and crossed the road with him, knowing she committed herself to the ride he had planned, and to the luncheon he had no doubt arranged. A car swooped upon them as they neared the middle of the wide road, and he gripped her elbow, pulling her near to him as the car roared past them. She was conscious of him as a tough, lean, attractive man. She felt in him an earthy tolerance for the person who strayed: he neither asked not expected a woman to be an angel. He was at once a comfort and a danger. He would make no demands, but he might expect this friendship to develop.

She glanced up at him as they reached the kerb. She would leave him now, before they reached the cab, but her resolve died away as the horse tossed his head and his beflowered harness jingled. What harm could come of a ride in the sun? It was as if she had half known it would happen, for her creamy dress with its spattering of scarlet poppies was an inexpensive summery thing she had bought last year in London. She felt wearing it that she retained some of her former self: the girl she had been before she found herself married to a man whose deep and unpredictable nature had her drowning in doubt, fighting currents that alarmed her, lost in rapture one moment, and swept by torment the next.

Other people's love lives had seemed so uncomplicated.

Nursing friends had met and married devoted young men who hardly disturbed the placid surfaces of their lives.

"In you get ... and may I call you Elvi, if only for to-day? I promise if we are ever in the company of other people I will be the essence of discretion and address you by your married name."

She met Raf's eyes as he assisted her into the cab, with its worn but comfortable seats shaded by an awning. She knew him to be teasing her, playing with her English shyness, and her sense of guilt in being here like this, a married girl with a husband who was jealous of his good name even if he wasn't jealous for love's sake.

"It would be a little ridiculous to be formal with a friend," she said pointedly.

He grinned lopsidedly and swung into the cab beside her. He called out something in Italian to the driver, who lazily swung his whip and set the horse in motion. They clip-clopped along this busy section, while cars and motor-cycles roared around them like angry bees. They passed the Fontana di Trevi, with its gods and horses and the water rushing down over the nymphs. "Have you been there yet to toss in a coin?" Raf asked, knees crossed as he lounged beside her, a hand resting lightly on his knee, revealing a carved ring that gleamed dully as old gold does.

"I thought only tourists to Rome tossed a coin into the fountain of Trevi." She watched as they circled the fountain and saw people leaning forward to watch the fall of their coins through the water; there was one young couple who clutched hands, honeymooners perhaps who hoped to return one day to the city of love. "You seem to forget, Raf, that I have come here to live."

"Ah yes, but even Romans are superstitious about the fountain. If about to take a trip away from Rome they visit the Trevi to placate its gods with a coin."

"What greedy gods," she smiled. "Don't they grant a wish without being paid for it?"

"Most things are paid for, in one way or another."

"Raf, look, the sunshine is free." She gestured with a creamy gloved hand that concealed her wedding ring.

"So it is, until it rains, and when it rains in Rome there are cascades from every slanting roof, every gable and church tower. Tiny Roman fountains spring to life everywhere."

"A rainy day in Rome sounds fascinating."

"It is, but everyone gets wet just the same."

"Really, Raf, spare me your logical Latin mind! I believed that Italians were the great romantics of the world, with their ancient ruins, their asphodels and arias. Not to mention the Titian faces one sees everywhere."

"Only a British girl could say a thing like that," he grinned. "Italian women are just good cooks. They can make spaghetti taste heavenly, but only a girl from England carries the tints of heaven in her eyes."

Elvi didn't move for several seconds after he said this, then abruptly she turned her head away and studied the Italian countryside through which they were ambling. "Where are we going?" she asked in a polite voice.

"Only a few miles to the coast. There is an old *trattoria* there built into the hillside, and after we have lunched we can go down to the beach . . ."

"Don't you have to get back to work?"

"Not when I take half a day off from work."

"Raf, I hope you don't think that I . . . want an affair with you?"

"Do you think I have affairs with every young woman I take to lunch?" He took her hand and held it lightly, reassuringly. "Are you afraid your dynamic husband will black my eye for daring to treat his young wife to a plate of roasted prawns and a bottle of wine, not to mention wild strawberries?"

"This day with you has got to be ... innocent. I love him, Raf."

"Lots of wives love their husbands."

"Don't say it so ironically, as if you spend your free time seducing wives. I ... I shall tell the driver to turn around."

"He has been paid to go all the way, and Italian cab-drivers can be very obstinate."

"So can English women."

"Obstinate and charming, and chaperoned by their innocence. Believe me, my face is a fraud. I am far less wicked than I look."

He said it so disarmingly that Elvi had to laugh.

"*Bene,* relax and enjoy the day. See, the sky is as blue as heaven, and there goes a doe running gaily through those woods, mad with the joy of summer." He broke into an Italian song and with gay audacity he sang as they ambled along these few miles of country road that led to the sea. They passed through a village of oriental-looking houses and steep, narrow, white-walled streets leading through a market place. They passed an olive grove, the foliage a mass of silvery green, the trees somehow ancient, twisted, almost forbidding, They symbolised the tenacity of the country people who toiled in the groves and wrung a living from the land.

Elvi breathed deeply the scents of the Italian countryside ... so different from the lush green meadows and wide ploughed fields of her own country. The sun touched her skin with a richer warmth. The scents were earthier, and the birds more like young hawks as they swooped upon the fruit that was already ripe in the orchards.

"*Ma che bellezza,*" Raf murmured.

"Yes, beautiful ... in a primitive sort of way."

"England is not primitive, eh?"

"No. Old, lovely, at peace with itself beyond the noise of the cities. Here in Italy the senses tingle all the time."

"Ah, that is quite a confession," he laughed.

"Don't get me wrong, Raf." She gave him a startled look. "I don't mean in the sense of wanting to be ... well, romantic all the time. It's more of a thankfulness to be so alive and aware. One bites at life here, as if it were a fruit."

"An apple?" he quizzed.

"Perhaps ... or a *pomodoro*." She smiled and felt the slackening of the tension that had seemed to hold her in its grip ever since yesterday. How true the maxim that a person with a secret should be careful to close his door. If Rodari had closed the door of his study ... oh, but she mustn't keep thinking about it. Like a sting it hurt again if she thought of it.

Today she would forget and enjoy this outing. The sun gleamed on the bronzy harness and hindquarters of the cab-horse, and the clopping hooves on the road was a holiday rhythm. As a child she had loved a day by the sea, and in Italy no one thought about *domani* until it came.

"That is better," said Raf. "Now the little nerve no longer tugs at your lip when you smile."

"I'm not used to playing truant, Raf. I was a very dutiful nurse."

"Did you say beautiful?"

"*No*, you heard what I said."

"And you intend to be an equally dutiful wife, eh?"

"Of course."

"I notice that he is very generous to you." Again Raf touched her hand, insinuating his fingers under the edge of her glove, where her bracelet lay. She had found it impossible to remove and had slept with it on.

At breakfast, as he sugared his grapefruit, Rodari had casually told her that it was an eternity bracelet. Once it was clasped about her wrist only a jeweller's tool could ever remove it. "It won't tarnish," he had drawled, "and looks very pretty."

"But –" It had suddenly felt like a slave chain about her wrist.

"But what, *cara*?" His eyes had held hers, their darkness unrevealing and stern. He had left for the studios shortly afterwards, and she remembered how she had stood alone in the hall, his brief kiss still alive on her hand, his touch still warm on her wrist, where almost deliberately he had pressed the ruby heart into the fine bones.

She became aware that Raf had pulled aside the cuff of her glove so that he might study the bracelet. "Gold, flesh of the sun," he murmured. "Rubies, blood of the earth. Hmmm, where does it unfasten?"

"It doesn't." She made herself speak lightly.

"I see." Raf's eyes travelled her face. "It is very *romantica* to carry your husband's heart on your wrist, and how it burns in the Italian sunlight. It's a gift in the Renaissance tradition, but then he always looks as I imagine Dante must have looked . . . or Machiavelli."

"That's enough, Raf!" She snatched her hand away. "If we're going to remain friends then I'd better warn you that I don't listen to insinuations about my husband."

"Is he everything a husband should be? Don't look angry. I promise to say it only this one time. The man whom a woman loves should be a friend and a god . . . a whiplash and a caress. Now tell me I am wrong, and that a woman doesn't want these things."

"Of course." She forced a smile, but the image of Camilla would not be forced from her mind . . . Camilla who must know the joy of being loved fiercely and exultantly by Rodari. "Every woman dreams of a many-splendoured love. I daresay men do the same. But love is not like a diamond that can be cut and polished to perfection."

"Or a ruby . . . ah, we are almost at our destination. Look, Elvi, we come in sight of the sea!"

The houses of the sea-folk clung along the harbour and

the sea wall, where the beach of shell sloped down to meet the sparkling water. Wooden breakwaters ran out for about half a mile, and fishing craft with colourful sails were clustered along the sea-front. There were wooden shacks smelling of fish, and the horse and cab made their way past them along a narrow track that serpentined upwards until they were above the harbour. The wind blew freely, carrying the salty tang of ocean and shellfish, and Elvi leaned from beneath the canopy to watch the blue and silver scene below, the jut of coloured sails, the green and scarlet coats of the trawlers, and the rugged men wading out to the boats and returning with loaded baskets on their dark curly heads.

"It's wonderful," she said. "Yesterday I attended a cocktail party with Rodari's sister ... eyebrows were raised as often as the glasses of Campari. I ... I felt like Cinderella and was afraid my fashionable suit would fall to ribbons."

Raf laughed and leapt from the cab as it came to a standstill in a courtyard that seemed cut from the rock of the hillside itself. A mass of pink oleanders spilled down the walls, and these supported wooden verandas and archways that led willy-nilly to all parts of the *trattoria*. It was moss-patched, delightful, beckoning ... and for a heart-stopping moment reminiscent of the café on the island, where Elvi had cared for Nicolina and her child.

She stared, pale and slender beneath the burning sky, and then Raf took her hand and led her inside. "*Cameriere,* a table for two," he called out, and they were shown to one that was shaded by a pergola smothered in grapevine. It seemed to Elvi they were romantically detached from the other diners, and waited upon with that extra touch of attentiveness which the Latin adds to a meal for two.

The menus were flourished, and Raf quirked an enquiring eyebrow at Elvi. "Shall we have big roasted prawns with lemon, crusty brown bread and butter, and a bottle of white district wine?"

"Sounds very appetizing," she agreed, for the sea air was beginning to whet her appetite.

"Sea truffles with the prawns," Raf added to the waiter.

"And to follow, *signore*?" The waiter held his pen poised above his order book, a dark eye upon Elvi as she removed her velvet cap and gave her head a little shake. Sunlight snaked through the vines and touched its fairness, cut short and softly waved above the pale slenderness of her neck. She had that fragile look of shy, quiet things, and when she glanced up her eyes held a pool-like quality. The softly burning dazzle of the jewellery on her hand and her wrist made her simplicity seem all the cooler ... that welcome coolness of soft rain on a warm day.

"You choose for me," she said to Raf. "I feel too lazy right now to study an Italian menu."

"*Bene*. I suggest veal cooked with marrow in the bone, and a salad of green vegetables. After that ride you must be feeling as hungry as I am."

"Yes, you are a sorcerer, Raf. If I had gone home to the apartment I should probably have made do with an omelette until ..." She broke off and watched the slow clenching of her hand on the table edge. "It's nice to be here. This sort of place appeals to me far more than the sophisticated restaurant."

"I thought it would." Having given their order to the waiter he sat back in his cane chair and studied Elvi. "You look very cool."

"Take off your jacket," she suggested. "Be informal."

"Why not?" He removed it and slung it over the back of his chair, and in his lemon polo-neck he looked even darker; the slant to his eyes and his cheekbones seemed to take on added definition. There was about him, without a doubt, a touch of the harlequin, but he was good company and never without a topic of conversation. It was curious that she should feel more at ease with him than she often felt with Rodari.

Their wine arrived a *bianco* with a sparkle to it. A twisty loaf had been cut into tasty-looking hunks, and a dish of golden butter was set beside the basket of bread. Their giant prawns steamed as they were served, the hot sauce redolent of lemons and herbs. The truffles looked a trifle odd, but they tasted delicious.

They talked of this and that over lunch, of Raf's career and his gipsy mother, and they laughed at little bits of nonsense. Elvi had the feeling that Raf rarely spoke of profound things. His spirit had a gay audaciousness about it, and he had an eye for colour and detail that had made him take to design. He had worked in the theatre as a designer, and he confided that London was his aim, where he hoped to run his own *salon*. London was now the centre of modern fashion, and he admitted freely that he was ambitious.

"You aren't a bit as I imagined male designers of women's fashion to be." She studied the puckish mobility of his face and she couldn't resist smiling. "Have you no family in Rome, Raf?"

"Do I seem to you a lonely orphan?"

"I am sure you manage not to be too lonely, but I have the impression that like me you have no close relatives any more."

"No one," he agreed, half mournfully. "Not even a sweetheart."

"Now you are straining my credulity," she scoffed. "You know too well how to please the female sex not to have your little book of telephone numbers."

"Do I please you, Elvi?"

"I have eaten all the food you chose for me."

"Now drink your wine," he coaxed, and he watched her over his wineglass as she sipped her wine. "Anyway, now you are married you have inherited a family, eh? You went to the family villa on the island ... tell me, what was it like?"

"Beautiful, mysterious, furnished with gracious Italian style."

"I hear that his mother was a flame-haired sorceress, and that she died tragically."

"Yes, Sabinetta died young."

"Like a flower, eh?" He leaned over and plucked a blue flower that grew with a cluster of others on a nearby wall. He presented it to Elvi, who put it to her nostrils and breathed the sweet, elusive scent. Suddenly she realised how far they were from Rome, and that if Rodari returned to the *palazzo* for lunch he would expect to find her there. She had told Amilcare she was going to have her hair done, so it might with luck be assumed that she had taken a stroll around the shops or had decided to do a little sightseeing on her own. It wouldn't do for Rodari to know about this cab ride to the sea. The other day at the fashion house he had seen Raf talking to her and had asked who he was. There had been a slight frown on his face. His shrewd eyes had noticed that the young designer was oddly attractive in the way some women liked ... the sort with whom seaside outings would not be approved by a husband.

"Elvi," a snap of Raf's fingers brought her back from her flight into panic, "you looked suddenly miles away from here."

"I was thinking ... Raf, we mustn't stay here too long. Rodari will wonder if I'm late home ... he'll want to know where I've been."

"Will you tell him?" Raf spoke casually, but there was an intentness about the way he regarded her.

"No ... I don't have to tell him everything, do I?"

"It is hardly a crime, Elvi, to spend a few hours with a friend, eating a meal, drinking a little wine, and getting colour in your cheeks from the sea wind."

"There is quite a wind blowing ... I hope the weather isn't about to change."

"The wind is always fresher on the coast. We will return to Rome, I promise you, after we have strolled beside the sea. Look how blue and inviting it is from this height."

She glanced down to where the sea glistened and in a flash she was reliving those nightmare moments on the island when the cliff had given way beneath Rodari and the struggling Nicolina. "Of course, Raf, we must go down to the sea."

"*Bene,* and before we go we will eat strawberries and cream like a pair of children. *Cameriere!*"

A laughter nerve tugged at her lip, for Raf was so irresistibly gay that it couldn't be wrong to be with him like this. When the waiter arrived with their strawberries her eyes opened wide with amazement. "They're as big as plums," she said in awe.

"Just eat them and don't analyse everything." He dipped a huge one in cream and ate it with relish. "Are you glad, now, that you didn't give way to your impulse to run away from me this morning, as if I had designs on your virtue?"

"You make me sound an awful little mouse."

"Not in the least awful, just a little timid, standing there on the pavement in front of the fashion house, being jostled left and right by the uncaring Roman crowd ... like Lygia among the lions. I felt I had to take you in hand before you became trampled on."

"That was gallant of you, Raf, but I'm not all that helpless." Strawberry juice stained her lips and gave them a full, almost provocative look. "I was a nurse, remember, and it's a fairly tough profession despite the blue and white uniform. Not all patients are brave and grateful. Some of them can be very difficult."

"I should have liked your cool touch on my burning brow, if ever I were ill, but I have always been blessed with good health and I carry a gipsy charm against accident." He sighed happily and lay back replete in his chair, his gaze upon her berry-red lips. "I think I was born under a lucky star ... gipsies are called the children of the stars."

"I think you have the gift for getting your own way."

He smiled unashamedly. "Yes, I have got you to myself, but admit you are enjoying yourself. Not a soul knows we are here, and when we arrive back in Rome I shall leave you before you reach home. I shall not tell anyone about today, and you can pretend that you have spent these hours roaming, let us say, through the gardens of the Caesars. Only visitors to Rome go there, so it will seem quite natural to say you have been there."

"I ... I hate to tell lies ..."

"Could you tell him the truth?"

She thought about it. "Only with difficulty. And now, *signore,* shall we take ourselves for a stroll?"

"Shall we take ourselves for a swim?" He leaned forward eagerly. "We can hire bathing suits and the water looks perfect. If you can't swim I shall teach you."

"I can swim. Mr. Clever." She gazed far down at the sea, blue and limpid as silk, and thought how cool it would feel rippling over her limbs. She had learned to swim when for a year she had worked at a seaside nursing home for young children. It had been part of her job to take them in the water and necessary for her to be an excellent swimmer.

Late one night at the villa she and Rodari had gone swimming in the lake. It had been exciting, part of the early rapture, the happiness torn too soon into shreds of doubt.

Hurt and angry again, she surrendered to Raf's suggestion. Why not? She could hire a cap and cover her newly coiffured hair.

He beckoned the waiter and settled their bill, and was informed that swimwear could be hired from the *trattoria*. Lots of people came there to dine, were soon captivated by the look of the sea and wished to bathe in it. If the *signore* and his *signora* would follow him? He drew back Elvi's chair and she arose without daring to look at Raf. She knew that the run of Italian men were curiously puritanical about marriage, so it was natural for the waiter to assume that a woman wearing a wedding ring should be the wife of the man with whom she dined. But it made her feel guilty, and it was only that nagging sense of rebellion against Rodari that kept her from grabbing Raf's arm and demanding that he take her home.

She still felt a bit tongue-tied when they made their way down the sloping stone steps that led to the sea-front. They had left their cabby dozing inside his cab, and carried beach towels wrapped around gaily coloured bathing suits. Their feet rang on the steps, for every sun-weathered shutter seemed closed against the hot stillness while the people inside the houses took their siesta. Everything smouldered with silence and scents, especially the smell of wild mint, which grew on long stems in the hot grass, powdered with fluffy seed heads. The cicadas mingled their harsh purring with the soft singing of the wind in the mastheads of the boats that bobbed lazily below the sea-wall. Boats of all shape and age, with their roped sails, their hung netting, their chains and figure-heads and coiled ropes. Drugged in the sun they rocked and whispered, and a salty haze seemed to hang over them. The water quivered under the caress of the sun.

Elvi stood by the low, rambling, waterworn wall, gazing from the sea to the old white houses that were built haphazard along the shore. Some of the gardens ended in the water, and beside a door stood the cart of a lemon-seller, shaded by a striped awning. The lemons hung in bunches on the trelliswork of the cart.

Everyone seemed asleep, they alone had escaped the spell that lay over the fishing village ... and then from one of the gardens came the sound of shears, cutting the silence. Elvi and Raf peered over the wall of the garden and there was an old woman pruning a fig tree and talking quietly to it while she worked.

"I wonder what she says?" Elvi whispered.

"There is an Italian saying that when the fig trees are budding the maidens should be locked up."

"I'm not a maiden."

"No." The lively, burning sparkle of his eyes met hers. "You are a safely married woman ... I almost forgot."

"Don't forget it, Raf." She ran on ahead of him across the beach. The tide was on the move and the sands of shell were beginning to go dark at the water's edge. Elvi went behind a beached boat and slipped quickly out of her dress and her underwear. Her bathing suit was a tangerine colour, and her cap was apple-green. She ran from cover with a spurt of laughter. "I feel like a lollipop in this gear," she called out.

Raf emerged, lean and brown-skinned in bathing trunks of gold. He struck a pose, and with a half nervous laugh Elvi dashed away from him in the direction of the water. The wind blew against her eyes and her throat, and then with a little gasp her body was yielding to the tingling caress of the sea.

"*Bello ... bello!*" She heard Raf come splashing into the water and with a gay abandon he began to swim and frolic about like a young porpoise.

"Race you!" she cried out, and at once he swam to her side and with a flash of white teeth he agreed and pointed to the far end of a breakwater, where the incoming tide was beating itself into a foam.

"Shall I give you a head start?" Raf asked wickedly.

"I don't need it, thanks."

"Then you had better not lose, because the loser pays."

Elvi laughed and trod water and prepared to launch herself at the ring of foam that marked the winning goal. "On your mark . . . get set . . . go!"

Her pale slender arms swung in unison with Raf's brown arms, and the way he grinned at her added to her determination to beat him. She knew from the amount of water he kicked up that he wasn't quite so expert as she was . . . nor did he glide through the water with the tiger-sharp expertise of her husband. There had been no getting away from Rodari. Each time she had tried she had ended up in his cool wet arms and beneath the waning moon, like a golden devil's horn, she had been kissed in the lake.

Lost in her thoughts, she didn't hear the motor-boat coming fast round the curve of the bay, whipping up furious spurts of water as it charged down upon the two swimmers, swerving away as the driver saw them, but too late for Elvi to dive beneath the waves as Raf had done. The thrust of the water tossed her like a cork and she whirled around helplessly and felt an awful choking sensation as the water lashed over her from the impetus of the engined boat. She struggled to get her breath as she fell through a sea trough, a slight swirling bundle of arms and legs. She felt she was losing her senses and somewhere in her dazed mind there arose the torturing thought that she was drowning and she would never again see Rodari.

Faces . . . scenes . . . they clamoured in her head as she was lost again in the crazy heave of the water . . . everything had been so gay only seconds ago, like two children playing, now everything was going so dark . . .

CHAPTER VIII

SHE felt so odd, and knew herself to be in a strange room. Sunlight, pale and cool, filtered through the ironwork of the windows and made patterns on the white walls of the bedroom. Her fingers clenched upon the kotted lace of the bedspread. Everything was unfamiliar . . . until her head slowly turned on the pillow and her hazy eyes met those of the person bending over her.

That stern-faced, black-haired figure was known in the deepest recesses of her soul. She had known him before meeting him, as if in another life . . . had he not said himself that long ago in the cloudy past she had been slave to his Roman?

"Hullo . . ." The word drifted from her lips, and when she spoke she realised that her lips were dry and tasted curiously of salt. She also felt a little squeamish and a look of distress ran across her pale face. "Something happened . . . I . . . I can't seem to remember what it was."

"You will before long." His arm slipped around her, warm and strong, and he lifted her into a sitting position. He put a glass of water to her lips and she drank eagerly, and wondered why she felt so silly and weak.

"I was so dry. . . ."

"And no wonder, after swallowing so much sea-water."

She stared at him, and she began to feel confused and afraid. His face looked . . . so hard. "Oh. . . ." Memory began to revive, and terror lived again in her eyes as she remembered in stabbing flashes the events leading up to this moment. "Did I almost drown?" she gasped.

"Almost." The eyes looking down into hers were so without expression that they seemed pitiless. "Stefano saved you and you were brought ashore in the motor-boat that caused all the trouble. You were put to bed here, after they forced the water out of your lungs, and Stefano then thought it prudent to telephone me. Lanciani brought me here in his helicopter. We arrived to find you still unconscious ... it was to say the least of it a bit of a shock to find my wife in such a state when I had thought her safely at home."

"I ... didn't see any harm in it ... t-to have lunch with Raf." Tears filled her eyes. "Y-you never seem to care very much ..."

"I care about my wife getting involved with another man." Above the angrily arched nostrils and the chisel-led cheekbones, Rodari's eyes now held small flames. "You always manage to look so innocent, yet I have only to leave you to go to my work and you land yourself in hot water. I could shake you, Elvi!"

"Please don't." She managed a shaky smile which she hoped might move him. "My head feels so funny ... as if it's full of cottonwool."

"You were given sedation to make you sleep the night through to get the shock out of your system."

"You mean it was yesterday when it all happened?"

"Yes." His eyes narrowed. "Your little adventure with Raf Stefano took place yesterday. I stayed here overnight. He flew back to Rome with Lanciani."

As she absorbed painfully all these facts her gaze dwelt on her husband and now she noticed that his chin was that dark blue colour from lack of a shave, and he was in his shirt with the tie pulled loose from his collar. He looked as if he had not slept a wink, and her heart quickened that he should spend a sleepless and possibly anxious night at her bedside.

"It was so very innocent ... like children playing in the sun. Rodari," she stretched out a hand to him, "do believe me."

"I am more inclined to believe that if you had not had your narrow escape from the speedboat you would have escaped less easily from your designing friend. I am told that he fancies himself as a Lothario."

"Don't most men?" she murmured, and her thoughts were crystallising as the haziness of the sedation cleared from her mind and she could think more lucidly. Rodari, of all men, to sit in judgement on Raf ... Raf who had saved her life!

"I suppose you would have preferred me to drown ... that would have saved you the embarrassment of admitting what a failure our marriage has been!"

"You are talking as if your head is still light." He rasped a hand over his unshaven chin. "You would not have been in any danger at all if you had not been persuaded by that smooth young man to go gallivanting." Suddenly, with a savagery that made her shrink against her pillows, Rodari leaned over her and curved a hand about the nape of her neck. "Do you think I like it, that the story of this escapade could have got into the newspapers if I had not pulled a few strings and made some threats? My wife in a seaside drama with another man! *Cielo*, you are shivering! Are you cold ... hot ... tell me!"

"I – I'm terrified of you," she managed to say. "Rodari, have you no compassion?"

He stared down at her and quite abruptly his face changed from a grim mask to become strangely haunted. "You must have a warm drink and something nourishing to eat. You feel you could eat?"

She lay testing her inward reaction to the thought of

food, and to her relief that queasiness had almost faded away. "I think so ... egg and toast would be nice."

"Good." He rose to his feet and picked up the telephone on the bedside table. He ordered a lightly boiled egg and toast for Elvi, and eggs and bacon for himself, with a pot of coffee and a jug of cream ... the freshest cream they had in the place. "For the *signora,* my wife," he added decisively.

Elvi lay in the soft spread of her hair looking at him, at a loss in her present weak state to deal with this abrupt change from anger to anxiety. What did he feel for her? What sort of an emotion was it that made him so savage with her when she had almost died? Could he not forgive her for being young and foolish enough to want a little friendship? Must she be friends with only the people he selected? Must she be a slave to his demands, while he planned to see Camilla again?

"Oh, Rodari," she sighed in her heart, "I didn't want to die because I would have lost you ... but, my strange darling, why do I care so much when you only care about your pride and your position? Why do I let you say these things to me when I know about Nicolina? When I have heard you speaking of love to someone else ... a love as inevitable as the stars and the tide?"

The waiter who wheeled in their breakfast was the picture of discreetness. Maybe because Rodari stood so tall by the sunlit windows, daring the devil himself to glance at the bed where Elvi lay.

"Leave the trolley," he ordered. "I will serve the *signora* and pour the coffee. You will, perhaps, ask the receptionist to hire a car to take us to Rome. In about two hours. That will give my wife time to be dressed and ready."

"*Si, signore.*" The waiter withdrew and closed the door almost silently. Rodari allowed himself a brief smile as he approached the food trolley and proceeded to dish

137

up their breakfast. The coffee he handed to Elvi, with about an inch of cream on the top, was like nectar to her parched throat.

"Delectable," she murmured. "I was dying for that."

He stood beside the bed with his own cup of black coffee and something stirred deep in his eyes as she used that word with lightness after coming so close to the reality.

"We will stay the remainder of the week in Rome," he said. "At the weekend we will go to Villa Corvina and you will stay with Elena and my grandmother."

"The Contessa?" she echoed, startled, a spoonful of egg halfway to her lips.

"Yes. If you are there I will know you are safe, at least. It may be a good thing. *La nonna* and I must come to an understanding now I am married and have a wife. The old wounds must heal."

"Rodari, don't you trust me any more?"

He bit deliberately through a crisp slice of toast. "Have you demonstrated that I can trust you? I don't wish to be called again to the telephone to be told my wife has suffered an accident. I have made up my mind. You will stay at my grandmother's villa."

"Have you considered that her attitude towards me could be similar to her attitude towards your mother?"

He drew in his breath, as if he felt a sudden pain. His eyes raked Elvi, slim and delicate in her lacy slip, her fashionable coiffure of yesterday now a confusion.

"I don't want to go where I shall be disliked ... because you order it. If you want me out of your way ..."

"I want you where I know you will be out of the reach of persuasive young Latins! Elena will be at the villa to keep you company, and you will be good for Elena. She needs someone young to be with, and you have too much spirit to allow *la nonna* to browbeat you. If she did so she would have me to deal with."

"She will try to bully me, when she hears why I've

been put into her custody."

"You don't imagine I will tell her about this escapade?" He quirked a black brow. "Eat your egg before it grows cold."

"*Si, signore.*" She bent her head and looked mutinous. "I suppose from now on I am to be treated like a truant child who must be kept under supervision?"

"Don't exaggerate." He leaned forward and coaxed a luscious piece of fig between her lips, and there was something sensuous about the gesture, a subtle indication that she was not a child to him. She ate the fruit and met his eyes, and she might in the next moment have been in his arms...

"I have to go on location with the film unit for two weeks," he said. "A few important scenes have to be shot in Sicily and as it's extremely hot there at present I wish you to stay at Corvina. You may charm that elderly autocrat who loves her own way so much."

"As you do," Elvi gasped. "You have everything your way. You marry me to satisfy a – a sense of revenge, and you think I can be treated like a Latin girl, someone just to take your orders and submit to your commands. The bride to tuck away in your grandmother's house while *you* go off gallivanting."

"Hardly that." He leaned forward and gripped her slim, shaking figure. "Stop all this emotion or you will make yourself ill. Come, be sensible. An Italian film unit on location is noisy, frenzied, and busy. We use locals for the scenes and this entails hours of coaxing, explaining, and bargaining. I would be working and you would be left alone much of the time..."

"To get involved with some other young Latin with designs on my innocence?"

"It has happened once, so why not a second time?"

"Why should you care, Rodari?"

"Because you are now part of the Fortunato name and

139

tradition. Our creed is faithfulness and an undivided heart."

"For the wives only, I take it?"

"What do you mean by that remark?" His eyes blazed into hers. "It is you, *mi amore,* who has strayed, not I."

"Not yet," she flung back at him. "You are waiting for the night of the Charity Ball, the secrecy of masks, and the memory of Venice."

"What the devil...!" His hands gripped, marking the pale skin of her shoulders, almost breaking her bones. "Elvi, the things in my past don't belong to our future ... do you hear me?"

"Yes ... I heard you." She twisted out of his hands. "I – I want to have a bath, and I have to dress. The car will be coming soon."

They left the *trattoria* an hour later and were driven swiftly back to Rome. Elvi sat in retreat in a corner of the car, watching the countryside flash by and feeling as if the events of yesterday had happened ages ago. Strange that something could be so terrifying, and then so soon forgotten. The reality, the centre of all her being, was Rodari himself. She fought him, yet in the end she surrendered herself to him. Nothing seemed to matter except her love for him.

She sighed ... if he felt such a love for Camilla then she could even understand why he still pursued her. Love dominated your heart and your actions; it drove you to do and say things you would never dream of with anyone else in the world.

"Are you feeling all right?" Rodari adjusted the rug across her knees; he had insisted upon that rug though the day was warm. "You have no sort of ache anywhere?"

She shook her head, and as her hand lay on the rug a flicker of sunlight caught the ruby and made it burn softly. It was only her heart that ached and there was only one remedy for that.

When they reached the *palazzo* she made the excuse that she was tired and would take a nap on the *chaise-longue* in her room. Amilcare brought her a light chicken lunch on a tray, and he had added a few flowers; a gesture which touched her. Like most good servants he was intuitive and loyal; he sensed that something dramatic had happened and he showed his sympathy without saying a word.

"Amilcare."

"Yes, *signora*?"

"Has my husband told you that while he's away in Sicily I shall be staying at the villa of his grandmother?"

"Yes, the *signore* mentioned this to me. The apartment will seem empty, *signora*."

"Yet I have been in Rome only a short while."

"There are some people who belong to Rome." He glanced around the bedroom. "This room was only for guests before the *signore* was married, then while he was on his honeymoon the interior decorators came at his orders and made this room as it is now. It is very suitable for you, *signora*."

"What guest used it before I came here, Amilcare?" She asked the question casually, her head bent to the flowers as if she breathed their scent, but inwardly she was tensed for his answer. She had to know; she had to suffer the ultimate before Rodari took her away from the *palazzo* and left her with the Contessa ... the woman whose autocracy had made his mother so unhappy.

"The *signore* has many friends," said Amilcare, hesitantly.

"I found a book, Amilcare, which had been left on the balcony. Did it belong to the guest who sometimes stayed here? I believe her name was Camilla."

"*Si, signora*."

Elvi glanced up slowly and met the rather unhappy eyes of Amilcare, torn between his loyalty to his master and his sympathy for the young *padroncina*, looking so slim and lost, curled in her robe on the silk lounger, her large eyes as if filled with frozen tears.

"It was only once that she stayed." Amilcare spoke in a low voice, as if he feared to be overheard. "The young Contessa was most unhappy and she came to the *signore* late one night. She was here when I came to work in the morning. I could see from her face that she had wept ... soon afterwards she was married to her *fidanzato*."

"I see." Elvi felt cold as ice and she clasped her hands about her cup of coffee. "Thank you for telling me, Amilcare. I – I had to know."

He bowed his head and then withdrew quietly from the room. Elvi heard someone speak to him in the corridor, and she tensed as the door opened again and Rodari entered the room, accompanied by a grey-haired man clad in an impeccable dark suit and carrying a small black bag.

"I have asked our family doctor to take a look at you." Rodari frowned slightly as he gazed down at her pale face. "My dear, this is Doctor Rossi."

She gave the doctor a bewildered look and he smiled reassuringly. "Your husband is concerned after your accident of yesterday and he wishes to be reassured that you are quite recovered."

"I – I feel fine," she protested.

"Well, I shall take a look and make sure." The doctor glanced at Rodari. "I should like to be left alone with your wife. Hovering husbands make *me* nervous."

Rodari, master of most situations, was not in command of this one and with a smile and a shrug he retired from the room and left Elvi in the hands of Doctor Rossi.

"So you have married one of my countrymen, eh?" Her hand was taken and while her pulse was checked her face was studied with interest by a pair of penetrating eyes. "Do you like Italy, *signora*? Or does it seem all very new and strange to you to be living here?"

"Doctor," she gave an exasperated little laugh, "I was a nurse before my marriage and I know I'm all right."

"It must have been a wrench for you to give up your career, and a change from being so busy to being a bride. The men of Italy don't care to have a wife who goes out to work ... if you would just open your robe a little?" The stethoscope was pressed to her heart, then to her lungs, and she was told to breathe deeply. "Hmmm, I think I shall give you some tablets to help clear that slight huskiness. We don't want you to develop an inflammation of the lungs ... your husband was particularly worried in case your accident in the water resulted in a pleurisy infection. His mother, as you know, died young following a similar accident, and Latin men are emotional in everything, even men such as Rodari."

Elvi tied her robe and felt the slight shake in her hands. All at once that sweet and startling smile lit up her face. "He was truly worried about me?"

"Most concerned." Doctor Rossi gave her a quizzical look as he made out the prescription for the tablets he wished her to take. "He rang me and insisted I come dashing over here as if you were about to give birth to his son. The good Lord help me when that day happens! He will demand my best nurses in attendance, buy a whole store of toys, and wish for the Pope to give the blessing." The doctor laughed and took a piece of fruit from Elvi's tray. "You would think some men married just to have a son."

"Perhaps they do, doctor."

The shrewd eyes swept over her. "Then such men should marry robust country brides. You will want to give him a child, of course?"

"If he wishes it, and I think he does." Her smile slowly faded, like sunlight going behind a cloud. "Perhaps that was at the root of his concern. Although he doesn't use the family title, he will want it to be passed on."

"The family is a very distinguished one in Italy. The Fortunato roots are in the Roman past ... take one look at him!" Then Doctor Rossi gave a chuckle. "But of course, you took more than a look."

"Are you puzzled that he should take more than one look at me, doctor?"

"Puzzled?" The iron-grey brows drew together. "I don't quite understand you."

"I am not a raving Italian beauty, nor am I rich or fascinating."

"You, *signora*, are fair and kind."

"Is it enough, for a Roman of distinction and power? You looked surprised when you entered this room and met me. Everyone seems to look like that and I begin to feel ... inadequate. As a nurse I knew my work and could be sure of not making blunders."

"These are early days." The doctor took her hand and studied the pale fingernails. "Are you *incinta*?"

She winced at the frankness of the question. "I don't know ... I could be."

"Would you be glad about it? Some women don't want a child too soon."

"It would hold him, wouldn't it, doctor? I would be the mother of his ..." She broke off before she spoke the word, seeing vividly in her mind's eye that baby boy on the island. Nico, with all the attributes of a child whose father was outstandingly attractive. She swallowed drily. Nicolina had not held him ... if he had fathered the baby.

Elvi put a hand to her bewildered head. A baby was so intimate a gift from a man. A child should be born of love. To grow up loved and sure of its place in the world.

"I will see you in a few weeks," said Doctor Rossi, clasping his bag and gazing with appreciation around her bedroom. "Are those Manet flower prints on your walls? And a Dégas ballerina! You appear to be a very pampered young lady."

She smiled at the doctor from her *chaise-longue,* and she looked in her silk-chiffon robe, with her hair softly fringed, and with rubies on her wrist and her hand, a sensitive picture such as Manet might have painted.

"Rodari is always generous," she said. "I want for nothing that befits the bride of a Fortunato. I should be crazily happy..."

"Love is not just for happiness. Love is for suffering as well, and trying to understand those we care about. Without its tribulations a marriage would become a bore. Without its winter the summer would not seem half so lovely."

Elvi's smile deepened. "I see you are a philosophical man, Doctor Rossi, and being also a Latin you put things in such a charming way. Thank you for coming to see me."

"It has been a pleasure, *signora.*" He took her hand again and this time he lightly kissed it. "I am a friend of the Fortunatos as well as their physician and available for another talk like this whenever you feel you need it. Your husband is a rather devastating man, and naturally you feel shy of him and wonder if you please him. You must please him ... you are married to him. *Arrivederci.* I may see you at the Villa Corvina. I visit the Contessa to check on her blood pressure and to play chess with her. Do you know Elena?"

"Yes. I like her immensely."

"She is a young woman who should marry again and have a couple of children. She has a warm heart and expends it on a lot of social work and the art galleries. Such a waste of an attractive person, do you not think?"

"Yes, but when you've loved very deeply ... it must be almost impossible to love again."

"Life is not very endurable without a love of some sort. Try to persuade Elena to accept some of the invitations she receives from young men. If she does not accept again the abrasions of loving she will become insensitive, a shape and not a real human being. Love cannot always give us the stars, but it can be companionable."

"I hope you have a rare companionship, doctor?"

"Alas no." He smiled broadly, but he seemed to be hiding behind that smile. "I am much too busy mending bodies and minds to have much time for marriage. Yes, I know what you are thinking! What a nerve I have to suggest that Elena finds a husband ... but Elena is a woman, and she has been married before. A woman is not quite so good at being alone, and one day the old Contessa will leave her all alone in that villa in the Sabine hills."

His eyes twinkled beneath the thick grey brows; a premature grizzling, Elvi decided, for his eyes were curiously zestful when he relaxed from his professional manner. "In the olden days the Romans took the Sabine women without pausing to listen to a lot of talk about life, art, and poetry. Those are all very nice, in their place, but ..."

He broke off in mid-speech and was shaking an amused head at himself as he made for the door. "I will inform Rodari that you are not as damaged as he feared. Rest for now. That man is rather overwhelming and I will tell him to leave you to yourself for a few hours. Goodbye again, *signora*."

"Goodbye, doctor."

The door closed behind him, and Elvi lay pondering his remark about Elena and the Sabines. Was it possible that Doctor Rossi admired Elena, not just as the granddaughter of the Contessa but as an attractive young widow? Hmmm, he obviously felt something, to talk like that about the abduction of the Sabines by the soldiers who had no women to wile away the winter for them.

She tinkered with her ruby wrist-charm. It was funny about love. Women did want it to be starry and everlasting; sweet, warm, and rapturous. But it was difficult to know about men. Did they confuse desire with love? Did they believe that a woman could share her heart and her body as they seemed able to share theirs?

Elvi could not envisage a sharing of herself with anyone but Rodari, and suddenly she wanted to see him, if only for a few minutes. She wanted to look at that dark and devastating face of his, and she wanted to believe that only *her* son would bear his likeness.

Amilcare came quietly in to take away her tray, and she asked if the *signore* was busy in his study.

"The *signore* has gone out for a short while, *signora*. He said that he would be home in time for dinner."

"I see, Amilcare." She strove to sound as if it didn't matter; as if her thoughts did not go leaping to Camilla. "I expect he has gone to the studios and that may mean that he'll be home late. You can go off early this evening and I'll cook dinner."

"*Si, signore.* There is a film I should like to see."

"Are you a film fan, Amilcare?"

He smiled, a kind and dapper figure in his grey alpaca coat. "It passes the time, *signora*. I enjoy very much the films adapted from the *padrone's* books."

"You are very loyal to him."

"Who could help it, *signora*? He paid all the hospital bills when my mother was so sick, and he arranged that we should have a nice flat not far from here. He is a very generous man."

"Yes, Amilcare." She fingered a pleat of her filmy peignoir, and alone once more she remembered all those stylish clothes owned by Nicolina; things she could never wear on the island, such as long glittering dresses and high-heeled dancing shoes.

Rodari was a good dancer, as Latin men so often were, with an inborn sense of rhythm. More than once Elvi had danced with him on the *terrazza* overlooking the lake, to music sweet and nostalgic. She shivered with the remembered ecstasy of being held close to his white jacket, feeling the crispness, breathing the tangy island air on his skin, crushed suddenly in his arms and carried all the way down the rough stone steps to the lakeside.

Looking back it seemed like a dream ... a dream of rapture torn and ravished by a typewritten letter and cash paid into a bank so that a child wouldn't want for the material things.

Her teeth bit down on the ruby heart. It felt as hard as his heart must be, if Nico were his child. She closed her eyes and visualised that small olive-skinned face, those big dark eyes, those curling lashes, the little chin that looked as if the very tip of a finger had made an indentation in the very centre of it.

"No ..." The word broke from her. "Oh, Rodari, no!"

At five o'clock Amilcare left for the night and Elvi set about preparing dinner. There were veal steaks in the fridge, plenty of tomatoes and button mushrooms, and she decided to make a casserole, which would not spoil if Rodari arrived home late. She sliced melon and ginger, and set out Rodari's old brandy and slim cigars. Then she went to her room and after taking a shower she dressed herself with care in one of the new dresses, delivered yesterday and hung with several others by Amilcare in the white closet with the louvred doors and the cedar-wood lining, inset with mirrors so she could view her appearance from every angle. The dress was a misty grey colour with an appliqué of tiny mauve flowers around the neckline and trailing the left side of the softly

148

pleated skirt. This was the dress which Raf had designed for her. . . .

Raf . . . she must ring him at the fashion house tomorrow and thank him for saving her life. She stared into the mirror into her own eyes. How did you thank a person for so big a thing? Words seemed so inadequate and Rodari had forbidden her to see Raf again.

She lifted her rosary from its case and clasped it about her throat. Rodari had taken the chain to a jeweller on the island and now the ruby-set clasp was firm and could not be pulled apart. Her fingers drifted over the chain of pearls; there were a hundred, she had counted them. A hundred prayers, once murmured by another woman long ago in a chapel plundered by a *condottiere*.

There her thoughts broke off as the telephone rang suddenly in the *salottino*. She hastened to answer it, feeling sure that Rodari was ringing to say he would not be home to dinner. She lifted the receiver and gave her name.

"*Carina.*" It was Rodari calling. "I am about to leave for home and Lanciani insists upon coming with me. Do you mind? Will dinner stretch three ways?"

"Of course." A smile of relief clung to her lips that he was coming home. "Amilcare always has plenty of food in store and I'll make a few more appetisers. Do you fancy asparagus?"

"Yes, among other things."

"Steak, I hope, with mushrooms?"

"Sounds *buono*. I think I will bring home a bottle of champagne."

"What are you celebrating?" Her heart seemed to give a little twist in her breast as she asked the question with mock lightness. Was he celebrating their imminent separation?

"Champagne is a tonic. Rossi told me that you were just a little off-colour and he thinks a stay at the villa will be good for you. Are you cooking the dinner?"

"*Si, signore.* I gave Amilcare the evening off."

"Sounds as if you wished to be alone with me?"

"No, I merely wished to use that fascinating electric stove with all the gadgets. Can I expect you within the hour?"

"*Si.* It is all right to bring Italy's most prominent film director to dinner? You don't feel it would be too much for you?"

"Rodari, I'm not an invalid. I feel perfectly fine, and it is about time I met the famous man. Is he enormous and booming, like Orson Welles?"

She heard Rodari laugh. "Wait and see. 'Bye for now." He rang off and Elvi stood gazing a moment at the silent telephone. Champagne and Lanciani, and all too soon a parting from Rodari that might last for several weeks. The soft chime of the clock brought her back to reality. She must see about the asparagus and the butter sauce, and lay another place at the table!

CHAPTER IX

ELVI heard the click of the key in the front door and she braced herself for this meeting with the director who was so widely known, and who was divorced from the English actress to whom he had been married for seven years. Elvi knew that film people were cynical about love and marriage, and seven years with one woman was considered quite a feat by those in the cinematic profession.

The door of the *salottino* opened and Rodari strode in, his eyes sweeping over Elvi as she stood by the balcony windows opening on to a view of Rome at dusk fall. Her dress seemed to reflect the sky at the turn of the evening, softly grey with its touches of mauve, and its little flashes of ruby and pearl. The soft fringing of her hair seemed to heighten the clarity of her eyes, and she wore a soft crimson lipstick to give her a touch of gaiety.

"Here we are, *cara*." Rodari seemed pleased by the look of her. "Do come in, Nick, and meet my wife."

Lanciani sauntered into the room. He was about Rodari's age, and at first glance startling because he almost resembled him, except that his skin was a lighter, more olive shade, as if he came from the south of Italy. He had a frank and inquiring Latin gaze, and a mouth boldly curved above a cleft chin. He wore a stylish summer suit, and carried an enormous cluster of deep purple grapes.

"I bought grapes, but I think I should have brought peaches." He smiled and his Latin eyes roved deliberately over her English skin. "I hope you are now fully recovered from your misadventure of yesterday?"

His smile was assured and he was undoubtedly handsome, but an instant flair of antagonism ran through Elvi. It was as if she looked through a glass darkly and saw a sinister reflection of Rodari. The impression was so strange and strong that when Lanciani reached for her hand to kiss it she retreated as if from the sting of a serpent.

"You are right, *amico*," he drawled. "Your English bride is shy . . . with me, anyway."

Rodari quirked her a look that was partly amused, and partly curious. Accustomed to seeing film-struck females bowled over by his associate, it struck him to silence for a moment to see the antagonised look in Elvi's eyes.

"I will put these here." Lanciani laid the grapes beside the bottle of champagne which Rodari had brought home.

"Thank you." Elvi forced a note of warmth into her voice. "I – I'll just go and take a look in the oven. Dinner should be ready at any moment."

She hastened into the kitchen and as she examined the contents of the casserole she could feel the quick, almost frightened beating of her heart. All along she had thought of the director as a big teddy-bear of a man, with a booming voice and an expansive genius. She could hardly believe in the reality. Strange that he should bear a sort of flashy resemblance to Rodari, who, thank goodness, didn't wear sideburns that slanted on to his cheeks, and a ring on either hand!

They were out on the balcony when she returned to the *salottino*. "Come and look," Rodari called. "The sun is setting and the sky is a feast of beauty . . . a carnival of the gods!"

She strove for self-possession and joined the two men on the balcony that seemed poised above the arena of Rome. The sunset over the city was like ancient fire; a flame and purple cloak sweeping with its hem the domes and towers that stood in black silhouette beneath the sun that died with such glory.

She felt Rodari's touch on her wrist, and when she glanced up at him his profile was etched imperiously against the pagan sky. "Rome is like a great theatre all set for drama," he said. "The evening sky is her back-curtain, and all of us her actors."

"This certainly is a great *pied-à-terre*." Lanciani lounged against the stone parapet of the balcony, and his strong even teeth flashed against his olive skin. "Balconies are so evocative, and a balcony overlooking Rome is so romantic. One thinks of Romeo and Juliet. Of Dante bewitched by a young girl's innocent face. What a pity you are a writer, Dari. On film your blue-blooded distinction and smouldering charm would make me a mint at the box-office."

"Don't worry, Nick, you will be a millionaire before you are forty." Rodari gave his deep laugh, with its hint of irony. "The people of Naples can never complain that their sons don't make a name and a fortune for themselves. But is a mint of money to be compared with a glorious sunset ... a laugh heard in the night ... a look caught in a pair of eyes ... a sail etched against sea and sky?"

"If I can get these things on to film, then I like them."

"But you don't notice them for their own worth?"

"Not skies or seas." Lanciani's gaze fixed itself upon Elvi; his eyes a stab of darkness against her breast, where the rosary half-hid itself in the misty-grey chiffon of her dress. "I am not quite so immune to more tangible charms ... *signora*, you much allow me to compliment you on your gown. It is simplicity itself, like the drapery of a fountain nymph that never falls ... but things so simple have to be well paid for."

Instantly, in a subtle and dangerous way, this man introduced Raf Stefano into the atmosphere. He had travelled back to Rome with Raf yesterday. He knew he worked as a fashion designer for Adalia, and that as a friend of hers Rodari would choose to buy his wife's clothes at her fashion house.

Elvi felt at once the pressure of Rodari's fingers about her wrist, the painful tightening and then the cool release. "Let us have dinner," he said. "The sun has gone down."

Yes, darkness had fallen over Rome and the many lights below were winking and burning along the boulevards. In the cafés and the gardens people were settling down to their food and their wine, and Elvi retreated into the apartment and set about serving up the dinner for which she had little appetite. Rodari opened the bottle of champagne, and over the surface of the evening there lay a brittle gaiety that held undercurrents of tension More than once Elvi surprised Lanciani's gaze upon her, and at the end of the meal he raised his glass to her, and his hair lay in a wicked jag across his forhead, startlingly dark against the olive-textured skin.

"To your eyes, *signora*. They are the colour of some grey amber I once found in a little shop in Paris. *Ambre grise*, in the words of the little old man behind the counter. He was a shrewd one because he made me pay his price. I showed too quickly that I wanted the amber."

He tossed back the glass of champagne, and when they entered the *salottino* for coffee and brandy he prowled the room with a restlessness that put Elvi in mind of the panther she had once seen in a cage at the zoo, when she was a schoolgirl. Nothing should be caged; she had thought, watching the creature, worried by its restless circling of the cage, its great tail switching, its eyes like cold but blazing jewels.

"Your coffee, *signore*."

"*Grazie*." Lanciani took the cup and stared into her

154

eyes. "Why don't you call me Nick, eh? Everyone else does ... well, nearly everyone. I prefer it to my first name, which is Roberto." He laughed as if at a very private joke. "It wouldn't do for me to be confused with that other master of the Italian film. Come, call me Nick."

"You should know by now," said Rodari, as he poured old brandy into lovely old glasses with deep engraved bowls, "that English women have a reluctance to be less than formal with a man on a first acquaintance. At the Alpine hotel where we met, it took a week for this child to call me by my first name. She can't yet bring herself to call me Dari."

"No," she said, her eyes raised to his as he came to her couch and gave her one of the lovely brandy bowls, the old gold of the cognac reflecting through the engraved facets like topaz. "I prefer Rodari. It suits you so much more than a curtailed name. It's very distinguished, and Dari is so youthful."

"But affectionate," drawled Lanciani. "Does your husband inspire you with awe and respect?"

"Like most ordinary people, *signore,* I bow my head to those who are gifted. When I first worked in a hospital I was always amazed by the sheer brilliance of the surgeons. As a woman patient put it, it isn't their youth that frightens one, it's their cleverness. I sometimes think that great writers dissect in much the same way as a surgeon operates."

"So clinically?" Rodari adjusted the knee of his impeccable trousers and sat down in a leather armchair; his lean hand cradled the bowl of his brandy glass, and his eyes held a deep glimmer of very adult amusement as they dwelt on Elvi.

"Oh no." She was almost shocked by that idea. "I don't mean ... it's just that you can take the heart apart with words, as a surgeon can with a scalpel. The best surgeons aren't cold, pitiless men. One at the National

Heart was a wonderful person. He would always spare the time to chat with his patients, and they loved him for it."

"There you are, Dari, you have not only a bride but an adoring fan."

Elvi glanced at Lanciani, detecting in his voice a mocking note, or was it an envious one because despite his faults Rodari was still a man a woman couldn't help but love? At the flick of the southern Italian eyes she bent her gaze to her brandy glass, looking into it to conceal the antipathy in her own eyes. Seeing Rodari in the company of Nick Lanciani was like seeing an original portrait beside a flamboyant copy. Like hearing thunder in the heavens, and then wincing from the unpredictable rake of lightning.

Rodari might be ruthless in some ways ... but instinct told her that Lanciani was far more so. Both men were gifted, but their inspiration derived from a different source. The film director came from the narrow byways of Naples. Clever, shrewd, and a gambler, he had probably used everyone he had ever known to gain him the possessions and the prizes he delighted in. The fame and the fortune; the beautiful and the brilliant. These were his court, and he set them high, their name in lights, or he brought them low.

Elvi wished he would leave. She longed for him to say that he must go, but he stayed on talking, of himself and the films he had made which had dared to speak a truth shunned by less daring film-makers.

"Love, the basic ingredient of life and films alike, is not a tender emotion, it's elemental." His arm slid along the rich dark leather of the couch and his prehensile fingers hovered tormentingly close to Elvi's shoulder. "It springs upon us like a storm. It can last for days, sometimes for years. A lifetime, or only a night. But, *cielo*, no man or woman has the right to demand that it be a

156

total sublimation from the moment it begins until it ceases to be. That would be a sheer bondage."

"It would take total love, my friend." Rodari flicked cigar ash into the tray at his elbow. "Perhaps a similar sort of love to that a nun gives to her calling, or a monk to his prayers. Not everyone can be so brave as to give so utterly but there are such lovers. Ah yes, Nick, despite your primitive belief in love for the sake of pleasure."

"It is a pleasure, *mio amico,* a million times more so than the rough robe of the monk and the stones of the cloisters." He laughed, and Elvi shrank physically from the brush of his fingertips. She was nervous, on edge, and she wanted to tell him to his face that he wasn't welcome in her home . . . but he was Rodari's friend. She was only the young wife who in a few days was being left at Corvina while Rodari went off filming with Lanciani on the island of Sicily.

"You must eat some of your grapes." Lanciani proffered the dish on which for the sake of hospitality she had arranged them. "Please me, or I shall suspect that you believe the old legend about a devil winking in every berry of the vine. Perhaps he does. They have such an alluring bloom . . . like the lips of women."

"You may eat all you wish, *signore.*"

"Is Nick not a favourite name of yours?" His eyes were devilish as he thrust a grape between his lips and burst it with a laugh. "We have wine and grapes, but no music. Come, Dari, as a *buon divertimento* why not sing for us? Did you know, Elvi, that your husband once sang for a sequence we did in Venice, when we filmed *The Princess Caprice?* Tell me, *amico,* do you plan to write a sequel to that story? It was a huge success for us, remember? We actually got away with a tragic ending to a love story."

"The sequel may end a little happier." Rodari smiled, and it seemed to Elvi that for a fleeting moment his eyes held a wistfulness almost boyish; a desire almost on the edge of tears. Her heart seemed to turn over. Venice ... a song of love in a gondola ... a lovely woman who knew she must marry another man ... the man to whom she had been given as a girl, in the old Latin tradition. What story could be more poignant ... and how could it end with happiness when both lovers were married to someone else?

"Come, you aren't the bashful sort, Dari. Sing for us *La Forza del Destino*. There is the piano. You have played and sung at studio parties, and I am certain your wife would enjoy the song. She has such clairvoyant eyes that she must believe in the force of destiny, the dictates of fate, the tears and terrors of life." His Latin eyes flashed to meet and hold hers, and those dark eyes seemed to say to her: "Yesterday was fateful, was it not? Had you been alone you might not have survived the drowning."

"Please sing," she begged of Rodari. "I never hear you do it seriously, only in the shower when you sound like a buffalo wallowing in water."

"*Mille grazie*," he rejoined. "No, tonight I am out of voice, and it grows late, and you are looking tired. Nick, it is about time you went home."

"To my lonely penthouse?" All at once the southern face was dark and sullen. "Have you heard the latest joke, *amico*? I still miss that red-haired, over-emotional creature I had the misfortune to marry. She had a damned magic ... Alice, what a name for an English witch! She should burn for walking out on me!"

"I thought love was a legend and bondage?" Rodari drawled.

"No, it's one hell of a desire, and that is all it is. I hated that creature, but sometimes I want her till I ache in every bone."

Lanciani climbed moodily to his feet, adjusted his tie,

slicked his black hair into place, and looked like a large disgruntled boy who had broken his own favourite toy.

He turned to Elvi. "I am grateful to you for tolerating me. Dinner was excellent, and I rather admire you, though you don't like me so very much. Strange how one senses these things, but with your eyes ... may I say of what you remind me?"

"So long as it isn't a daisy," she retorted. "It has become a cliché, if one is plain and a bit shy."

"Plain?" He raised an eyebrow very slowly. "The bride of Fortunato? Listen! '*And down the long and silent street, the dawn, with silver-sandalled feet, crept like a frightened girl.*' That is how you seem to me, with words by Wilde."

"Come, you reprobate." Rodari stood with a hand lightly in the pocket of his smoking-jacket. "Don't waste your wiles on Elvi. She has no ambitions to be a film star."

"What a pity, with those eyes. They have something of the Mona Lisa in them, a hint of Garbo, and secrets of their very own. She would make a perfect Héloïse, or a Beatrice. Beatrice on the bridge as Dante passed by and fell a mortal to an immortal love."

He strolled to the door. "*Buona notte, signora.* What a shame you are not coming to Sicily."

She stood staring at the empty doorway and heard the drift of Italian from the front door. The aroma of cigars lingered in the *salottino,* the dregs of brandy lay in the engraved bowls, the little shafts of the conversation had left their mark on Elvi. She felt suddenly an emotional fatigue that made her sink among the cushions of the couch, her head at rest against the vari-coloured silks. She awaited Rodari, submissive in her weariness, with no will left tonight to ask him to take her with him to Sicily. She couldn't plead with him, yet she had the feeling that something was going to happen to their marriage.

It was almost tangible, like a pain, a tugging at her heart and her nerves. Take me with you, her nerves were crying, yet when he returned to the *salottino* she lay curled among the cushions as dumb as if she were a doll, a mere distraction which he could tuck away from the more serious aspects of his life; a pet he could dally with and then forget.

He stood gazing down at her, a slight smile on his lips. "You found Nick difficult to like, eh?"

"He is a bit overwhelming," she agreed. "Has anyone else ever commented on the fact that he resembles you, in a flamboyant sort of way?"

"Lots of Italian men bear a resemblance to one another; it's the darkness of the hair and the eyes, a certain something about the way we look at a woman. Do you mind that the Latin male appreciates the fact that a woman is different in every way from a man? His opposite in body, soul, and sensitivity, yet his counterpart, his completion, and his comfort?"

"Your director seems a very troubled and mixed-up sort of Latin. Rodari, is that why you give him your friendship? I should imagine he finds it easier to make enemies than friends. The way he spoke about his wife! As if he possessed her and would never forgive her for daring to leave him. They must have fought like tigers."

"Yes, and someone has to try and keep him reasonably tame. In his way he's something of a genius, and I have my reason for letting him come here. Because Alice left him, he no longer believes in the existence of goodness or happiness. I hope to make him see sense, before it's too late."

"But he seems to want only money. You said he'd make a million before he was forty."

"He probably will, but there is something else he must be persuaded to do."

"Settle down?" Elvi smiled at the idea. "Perhaps with

a harem of film-struck girls. Rodari, one has only to look at him to see he's a devil."

"But so am I." Rodari sat down on the couch and rested an arm across Elvi's slender figure; his eyes held hers, dark as night, yet with a flicker of soft-burning flame deep within them. "You have told me so on more than one occasion."

"Yes . . ." She ran her eyes over his lean and autocratic face, seeing there no trace of the vanity, the self-indulgence, and the avarice she had seen in Lanciani. Rodari's devil was linked to Camilla . . . to a broken love leading to Nicolina. "You are subtle, Rodari. I don't know the person you really are. I only know your touch, your kiss, or your anger when I do something like almost getting drowned and dragging you away from your work."

"Poor child, let me make amends." He bent and brushed her lips with his. "You feel fragile, and the heat of Sicily can be fierce. Elvi. . . ?"

"Yes, Rodari?"

He drew a little away from her and he did not touch her with his hands, only with his eyes. His gaze was electrifying. She felt in him the conflicts of his nature, and the strong desires . . . vibrations as vibrant as his pulse beat. Her cheeks as he looked down at her took slow fire . . . did he think that Doctor Rossi had found her with his child?

"Elvi, don't ever keep secrets from me."

"You are the one with the secrets, *signore*."

"I am a Latin, and I am older than you. I am your husband."

"And I must take your orders?"

"Are my orders so severe? If I leave you at Corvina I do it for your own good, and I give you these." His hand came from his pocket and his fingertips were alive and warm at her earlobes. "Stay as you are and I will fetch a mirror."

161

He arose and fetched a scrolled Venetian mirror from off the wall. He held it so she could look at herself, reclining like his slave girl, ruby drops burning against her earlobes, set in exquisite gold filigree, antique and utterly Italian.

"Oh!" She caught her breath and touched them with her own fingertips. "They are beautiful, like tiny living flames. Rodari, you are so madly extravagant, but I do love them."

"They suit you, so warm against your white skin." He laid aside the mirror and reached for her with his lean, sure hands. She felt his touch to her bones and had the startled thought that he would like to crush her, to make her cry out, as the tortured do at their moment of agony. What then would he hear? Her cry from the soul that he admit or deny he had already a son from another girl!

"How do you thank me?" A steely arm swept round her and held her. "Come, wench, what in return do you give me?"

She lay there with her head cradled against his arm, with his face only inches from hers, so utterly his that it was frightening. Never had she been so aware of love as a living force, beyond reason, and doubt, and the knowledge that he had taken her into his life because he was a passionate man who could not live alone. Her hand weighted by his ruby clenched upon the thick silk of his shirt, and there was his heart, beating at her fingertips. She was this close to him, yet always Camilla stood between them.

"What would you like?" she asked. "I have no money of my own, and you have expensive tastes, *signore*."

He stared down into her grey eyes and a thread of a frown joined his black brows. "I don't ask from you the things that can be bought with money."

"But you give them, Rodari. The best clothes, fabulous jewellery, a room furnished with lovely things. You ...

you never needed to buy a bride."

"Don't I give you what every woman wants?"

"The material things."

"Say it isn't pleasant to catch the admiring eyes of another woman upon your dress and your jewels."

"And upon my husband?"

A slow and teasing smile crossed his face. "I think sometimes you like being the bride of Fortunato. My girl-wife who looks as if she believed in and was part of all the myths about cloud-lovers, sun-gods, and offspring from the rain."

"Don't be cruel, Rodari!"

"This is cruel?" His lips explored the side of her neck, and she felt the responding leap of all her senses. Did anything matter except this? The kisses that closed her eyes, the hands that caressed, the heartbeats like a soft thunder.

"No ... no." She twisted her lips free of his. She wouldn't surrender to the bitter-sweetness ... she wouldn't share him again with those other women. "Rodari ... no ... don't touch me!"

He drew away from her and his eyes were leaping with a dangerous fire as he looked at her, studying her face with its look of torment. "Can't you bear any more to pay for what I give you?" he asked, and in that moment his face had a cruel beauty. "My dear tortured angel, please don't look at me like that. Console yourself with the thought that I shall be away from you for two whole weeks ... in fact we might as well go to Corvina tomorrow, then you won't have to spend any nights alone with me, apart from tonight. And all at once tonight I have a desire to go and work in my study."

He released her and rose to his feet. He buttoned his smoking-jacket and shot a look at his wrist-watch. "Go to bed, *cara,* and try to sleep. I shall not disturb you. *Buona notte.*"

He swung on his heel and walked out of the *salottino.*

163

A moment later she heard the door of his study close behind him, then all was silence. She felt the hot, weakening attack of tears and fought against them. They burned in her eyes, ached in her heart, for she longed to run to him with the real and agonising truth. It wasn't his touch she could not endure; it was not knowing if her love was given to Nicolina's lover.

She plumped the cushions of the couch, turned out the lights of the *salottino* and carried to the kitchen the brandy glasses and the ashtray. She washed and dried them, ensured that everything was in order for Amilcare in the morning, and made her way to bed. She passed the study, but could not hear the typewriter clicking busily beneath the long fingers. She paused by the firmly closed door and had a vision of Rodari standing tall and haughty by the windows, staring at the night sky and watching the stars, those winking eyes of gold that gleamed and closed, shone and slumbered. Or was he slumped in his huge swivel chair with the leather headrest, in which she had once sat and felt lost? She remembered each detail of the room in which he wrote his famous books.

The bold Italian desk decorated with carved figures, the ruby-glass lamp on one corner, and the Borgia wine cup upon the other, with a gleaming facet that could be pressed open so poison could be dropped into the wine. A large typewriter covered in black alligator stood always ready for use, and the panelled walls held groups of fine paintings for the eyes to rest upon. It was an austere room, and yet attractive, with the files and notebooks and recordings of a writer's work concealed in the antique cabinets with their fine ormolu finish. The carpet that covered all the floor was a deep rich crimson to match the curtains.

For Rodari that touch of warmth and passion was necessary. It was part of his nature, smouldering under the distinction, the natural authority, the air of intellect. It was a vibrancy and a fascination that could make a woman forget everything when he took her into his arms.

It was a dangerous gift, for it enabled him to be loved and forgiven too often, and Elvi had to find the strength – perhaps when he returned from Sicily – to ask him about the child on the Isola Fortunato; the boy with the dark-lashed eyes and the promise of a cleft in the very centre of his chin.

More than once had she left a kiss within the cleft of Rodari's strong Roman chin.

CHAPTER X

THEY were driving into Sabine country, the wild and lovely land beyond the city of Rome, where fields of rape shone like copper under the sun, and ditches and streams were flooded with flowers. The fabric of the day was golden and flawless, with vineyards veiled in vines and orchards silvery with olives. There hung on the air the heavy, sensuous scents of summer, and Elvi's hair blew against her cheek as they drove along with the hood of the car open to the sky. Madonna blue, unclouded, promising fine weather for days to come.

Days that would be empty – though not half so empty as the nights – because Rodari would not be at the Villa Corvina to share them with her.

She stared at the hands upon the wheel of the car, sure and strong, the nails clipped and spotless, the lean fingers without even a signet ring. A tiny secret tremor ran all over her skin, for those rather beautiful, rather ruthless hands had known her with strength and surely with pleasure. Had he not whispered, in the Italian she was learning so well, that her skin was like the softest silk? But how many times had he whispered those words to those other women? How often had they thrilled to his touch and his flattery?

Elvi clenched her hands on the chain of her handbag. She looked at his profile and found it still and remote. She remembered their drive through Tuscan country the day of their marriage. Then as now she had been afraid of the future. Oh, if only she could say the words that clamoured in her mind! Rodari, which of us can make you truly happy? The Contessina whom you loved in Venice? The pretty island girl whom you found in Rome? Or the English nurse you met in the Alps, who seemed in her shyness unusual, who ran from you the first time you touched her. She fled down the snowy slopes and you pursued her. You were dark and strong against the pallor of the snow, Apollo in pursuit of the nymph, with not a laurel in sight for her to hide in. A tiny, irresistible smile tugged at her lip, and it was then that Rodari glanced at her.

"Why are you smiling?" The question leapt, startling her. "Are you contemplating with delight the prospect of being without your demanding husband for the next two weeks?"

"No . . . really. I shall miss you."

"I hope you won't behave like an impulsive child again. Sicily is a bit further away than Rome, and you might feel tempted."

"I am sure your grandmother will keep an eagle eye upon me. I have the feeling she is a stricter guardian of the family honour than you are."

"And may I ask why you have such a feeling?"

"The Contessa is a woman. You, *signore,* are a man, utterly and without the slightest fraction of a doubt."

"You sound in a flippant mood, *cara.* I believe you are looking forward very much to my departure . . . don't dare to deny it! Last night was an indication of your feelings. As an English girl you don't like to be dominated. You were not brought up to the idea of belonging so exclusively to a man. You resent some of my Latin ways. You have thoughts, feelings, and secrets you don't wish to share with me, and I must accept and have patience with your reserve. Forgive me a little, if I have been impatient with you. In most Latins there is this tendency

167

to look upon what is theirs as something another man is bound to fancy."

"Such as this dashing car, Rodari? I am sure I fall into the same category, along with the acres of land upon which the Villa Corvina was built, over the ruins, no doubt, of a Sabine farm sacked by a Roman who must have looked and behaved exactly like you."

"How do you mean . . . behaved?"

"I have read the history books, Rodari. The unprotected Sabine girls were carried off like chickens by the Roman soldiers, their struggles and implorations merely laughed at. Women have feelings, you know. They aren't just objects and playthings."

"*Cara*," he laughed lazily, "heaven forbid that the day should come when woman ceases to amuse and gratify. All this talk about equality is so much nonsense. How is any woman equal to a man when she can be so fair and delightful? When she can smile to move the heart, and give birth to a small creature who actually resembles the large, stuttering, awestruck male who stands at her bedside and wonders how such a miracle was accomplished by a slip of a girl he could so easily break in his two hands. Equality, my child? There is no such thing. There never can be. Woman holds the secret of life in her body, and if man chases her, and takes her, it is because he wants life perpetuated. It is the primeval instinct in him . . . and if I remember my history books correctly, the Sabine women became quite fond of their Roman warriors and did not return to the farms to take care of the livestock."

The car as he spoke turned off the main highway on to a narrow road that was rough beneath their wheels and which seemed to cut through the fields as if it were a private road. For the space of seconds Elvi was disarmed by his words, and then their full meaning seemed to explode in her brain. Was he actually telling her that he had experienced a feeling of awe at seeing a child who resem-

168

bled him borne by a mere girl whose heart he had broken? Her own heart felt as if it were a bird, beating wings inside her; wild, caged wings.

Now as they drove the hills arose on either side of them, shaggy with grass and freckled by wild flowers. Now and again there was a clang of goat bells, and then abrupt solitude broken only by their engine. This was the kind of landscape the Italian masters had put upon canvas, unchanged down the years, the centuries. Here indeed, in these very fields, had the Sabines run screaming from the soldiers, who without mercy had snatched them away from their rustic surroundings and carried them off to rough tents, where armour glinted and the smiths at their forges hammered the broad swords and the breastplates worn by their ruthless, laughing, handsome masters. The men who conquered, and came home to make love to their captive country girls.

The landscape was brown and silvery, with clusters of chestnut trees growing on the verges of the farmhouses with their red-tiling and their painted shutters, their shadowy archways where the animals were stabled, and their stone stairways leading to the family rooms. Old, historical, and evocative.

Asphodels, blue as tiny chinks of heaven, bloomed in the sunburned brass. A heavenly day . . . but dark, torturing, were Elvi's thoughts.

Perhaps it was symbolic that stately cypress trees, with their dark foliage, should stand sentinel along the drive leading in shafts of sunlight and shadow to the Villa Corvina.

They came to it suddenly, around a bend in the drive, and it had a dignity, a slumbering Italian beauty that struck painfully at Elvi's senses, arousing a response she had sworn not to feel. Shattering the oath she had taken to love nothing more pertaining to this man at her side, this arrogant devil whose staggering attraction made him a law unto himself. A man who could take and toss aside. Talk and write like an angel, and yet abide by none of the things he wrote about.

The car slid to a halt at the base of the stone steps leading to the villa. The engine was silenced, the air was still and hot, and Elvi felt that she couldn't breathe.

He had turned and was looking at her, dark and handsome in his cream jacket, brown silk shirt, brown trousers, and shoes of elk-thong. He was assured, worldly, elegant. He was her husband, and she wanted to hate him, but was overborne by the treachery of her own senses. She wanted to strike him for making her love him even as she hated him. She wanted all of the truth from him, all that lay in hiding in his heart, and then she felt his hands taking hold of her and the hot, aching words shrank away into their hiding places.

"Don't look at the house as if it were a prison," he said. "In a few minutes Elena will arrive to greet us, so please look as if you are glad to be here."

"Is it an order, that I look madly gay and glad?"

A swift frown struck the smile from his face. "I am merely suggesting that you don't give the impression we have quarrelled and I am leaving you here as a kind of punishment. Elena will be hurt because she likes you, and the Contessa will be gratified to see the signs of her dire predictions written in your eyes." He gripped her chin with his hand and held her face up to his. He searched her eyes and his frown slowly darkened. "Right now, *cara*, your rebellious eyes seem almost to hate me. Why? Because I discovered that you can deceive me with another man? Because I broke up the little game you started to play with that almond-eyed young man?"

"Yes, if you like," she said recklessly. "Raf was rather charming, and he saved my life."

"Only after he had almost caused you to lose it. He was reckless to invite you to the sea. As a Latin he knows how dangerously an Italian husband can react to a situation like that, no matter how innocently his wife may have entered into it."

"I am gratified, Rodari, that you still believe in my innocence."

"Be thankful that I still believe in it."

"I suppose by bringing me here you are making sure that I remain chaste and unchased while you are away." She spoke with the flippancy of her deep hurt; of knowing that he expected angelic behaviour from her without the least intention of being a saintly husband in return. The great dark pupils of her eyes seemed to fill with his lean, imperious, Roman face, and her own impulses were hateful to her. How could she ache with love of him when she knew him to be the dark and secret lover of Camilla ... the man whose initial was slashed like a knife cut on that heartless letter which Nicolina kept under her pillow in her room beneath the eaves of the sun-weathered café on the island.

"Look at the house," Rodari commanded. "Does it look such a prison?"

The façade was strikingly old and lovely, built from stone which had taken to itself the tint of the sun. Fuchsias and oleanders spilled from stone containers, the balustrades and balcony fronts were of scrolled iron, and lamps delicate as big glass jewels stood at either side of the great carved door. There was an air about the place of having seen gay and romantic times; now it slumbered in the sun, as if it waited for the sound of laughter, the echo of young voices, the rustle of silk against the stone, the love that brought all houses alive, whether they were old or new.

Its beauty was baroque, timeless, with a steepled tower attached to add to the sense of enchantment. The columns of the porch were dressed in vines that climbed to the balconies and smothered them in a green, flower-starred cloak. Cicadas could be heard in the old classical gardens that lay on the other side of the walls.

No, not a prison, but a house that twisted the heart within Elvi because all her life she had dreamed of such a place and now it came to lazy, sun-drenched life in front of her eyes. Her impulse was to love it, at first sight, but so had she loved Rodari, and such love could hold a painful disenchantment.

"Well?" His fingers tightened on her chin and she gave a tiny gasp of pain. "Do you think I intend to lock you in the tower, with only your embroidery to keep you entertained?"

"I never learned how to embroider."

"Really? I thought all women were adept at it, especially where the truth is concerned. Surely they can strand their silks to form whatever pattern suits them?"

"Please stop this!" She twisted free of him just as a slim figure came out of a leaf-hung side door. Elena in dark slacks and a cream shirt came hurrying across the forecourt to greet them. Her face was lit by an eager smile. "It was such a lovely surprise when you phoned, Dari. I suppose you have to go off to Sicily right away?"

"You sound as if you will be glad to see the back of me?" He spoke drily as he swung out of the car and reached into the back for Elvi's suitcases.

"It isn't that," she said, tucking her arm into Elvi's with a touching friendliness. "I'm not wishing you away, but it will be fun to have Elvi's company while you are busy with the film, and Sicily can be a bit of a furnace, especially for someone from England, that cool, green place."

"Really!" Elvi had to laugh as the three of them made their way into the villa through the side door. "We do have a certain amount of sunshine in my country. It has been known to reach seventy-five degrees, and a London hospital can seem pretty hot when that happens."

"Sicily has earthquakes," said Elena, as if that fully explained Rodari's reason for leaving his wife at this attractive villa outside Rome. "Well, *sorella mia,* what do you think of Corvina? It has the reputation of being one of the prettiest houses in Italy. I love it, of course, but one is always a little blind to any faults where love is concerned. *La nonna* calls our tower an illegitimate offspring, but it was part of the old castle that once stood on this land and was kept intact when the villa was built. Both the tower and the villa are built from Italian stone, so they have attained a similar colour down the years." Elena gave a little laugh. "Like an older husband with a young wife. As time goes by they seem to take on a blending of tones, a similarity of style, a closeness that makes them seem as one."

Elvi shot her a startled look. Did Elena believe that time would bind herself and Rodari so closely together? Yes, she was a romantic creature. It would shock her deeply if she knew the truth about the brother with the distinguished looks and the gift for great writing. They might tease each other, but she was obviously proud of him and the name he had made for himself in the world of letters. The smile she gave him in that moment radiated pride and love, and Elvi caught her lower lip between her teeth, checking her little gasp of pain. At the start of their marriage she had been able to look at him with unclouded eyes. She had felt so unbelievably proud, even though her knees had trembled, when they had knelt side by side on the scarlet cushions in the chapel, and the candle-flames had sheened his hair. "My husband," she had thought. "This tall, upright, famous man has just murmured in Latin that body and soul I am his to cherish."

To cherish! Surely the most lovely and perfect word ever spoken?

Feeling a little dazed, she glanced around the hall of

the villa and found it as romantic as the outside. The ceiling was a series of frescoes that seemed carved and then brilliantly painted, as only the Italian artist could paint, using colours of enamelled clarity and tone. The ceiling was supported on columns held by sculptured stone figures, the floor was marbled, and arched alcoves held brocaded sofas, elegant vases, and large mirrors in gilded panels. The entire effect was splendid, and a touch of delight was the folly at the foot of the great branching staircase, like a big bird-cage in wrought-iron, with a dome and twining leaves and flowers.

Elvi, in her white dress with a scarlet scarf at her throat, had the feeling that she was out of place in these utterly Italian surroundings, while Elena and her husband were perfect, like figures who had stepped down from that mythological ceiling, their Latin features and expressive eyes, their raven brows and hair so right and so eye-catching.

It was no wonder that Italian painters had always been so good. They had never lacked for inspiration, not with such faces to put upon canvas, and such a landscape as the olive slopes and lemon gardens of Italy, and the cities so evocative of intrigue and passion.

It was in that moment that Elvi realised fully her love of this land, to which she had come a stranger, and a bride. It would be unbearable if she ever had to leave this April land and the azaleas in glazed bud. The oleanders burning with colour in the hot sunlight. The honey skin of the children, and the keep dark eyes. The heavy scents, and the coolness of the chapels. The velvet night ... the sensuous delight found here in warm old walls, the bloom on fruit, the discovery that Italians were rich in soul and subtle in the ways of love. A mingling of the saint with the satyr.

She gazed at a vase of madonna lilies, standing there like the trumpets of angels waiting to be blown. She felt herself to be young and defenceless, and soon to be abandoned by Rodari to his grandmother the Contessa di Fortunato.

She gave a little shiver, and then realised that Rodari had come across the hall to where she stood near the folly of scrolled iron, and he was studying her with a faintly ironical smile on his lips. "We don't keep birds in it, or brides," he drawled. "Though it certainly looks big enough to hold you. Why, Elvi, do you seem so little and lost today . . . ah, you are wearing low-heeled shoes! For a moment you made me feel oversized, like a giant about to eat you."

Her eyes dwelt upon him, sliding to the wide shoulders that when touched by her hands had the smoothness and strength of steel. She felt a curious sensation of weakness. Soon, now, he would say goodbye, and he would drive back to Rome to catch his flight for Sicily. She didn't want him to go, yet if he stayed the tormenting doubts would go on, and when he touched her again she would shrink away, as if from a ravishment of the love inviolate in her heart. She wanted all of this man, and it was unbearable to have but a third of his heart.

"My country shoes," she quipped. "A girl can't climb the hills and byways wearing smart city shoes. I may even run about barefoot like those other Sabines."

At once his smile took on a subtle danger. "You may play at being a Sabine, but you will wait until my return for the game to be finalised. The air in these hills is like wine, so beware. Act the child by all means, but I want none of that impetuous behaviour of the other day. In England it might be acceptable for a young, newly married woman to have a friend of the opposite sex, but here in Italy the people are not so liberal in their views. Marriage is more sacred."

"Is it, Rodari?" She gazed at him with eyes that might have looked cynical, if they had not held a clouding of pain and perplexity. "I expect you mean there is one law for the men, and another for the women."

"The man is the master, if that is what you mean." He arched a black brow. "Or are you being feminine and illogical?"

"The two would merge as one in your masculine mind, wouldn't they?" She contrived a smile and glanced over to where Elena had stood talking to him. His sister had now disappeared, and instinct warned Elvi that she had gone to fetch the Contessa. Nerves tightened along her rib-cage, as if to hold like a bird her quick-beating heart. Nerves tingled all through her as Rodari took hold of her and bent his head as if he meant to kiss her. She twisted her head away. "No ... your grandmother is coming!"

"She is aware that we are married! Why the sudden coyness, Elvi? Why the air of retreat? Are you trying to punish me for some misdeed? I warn you, *mia*. I won't tolerate the sulks, and if you are not careful, *la nonna* will discover you being spanked instead of kissed."

"I ... I'm sure it would delight her. Brides should be kept in their place, shouldn't they? The bedroom and the nursery!"

At these words his hands really gripped and bruised. Elvi could not contain a cry, and the Contessa must have heard it as she entered the great hall on the arm of her granddaughter. Elvi at once wrenched free of Rodari and stood gazing at his grandmother with almost the air of a creature pursued and trapped in a gilded cage. Her eyes were immense in her pensive face as she met the woman who long ago had caused Sabinetta to run away from her husband.

She was elderly but still patrician, elegant with her blue-silver hair, and her silk suit with a stiff lace collar. Her face was sculptured by the ancestral past, lined by the years and the sun of Italy. Her rather thin lips were painted, and she wore black pearls in her earlobes, and rings set with diamonds and black pearls. There was something of an aged Messalina about her. Her dark gaze was still dominating. She was obviously a woman who had enjoyed much power through her life and who still exerted it. The way she hung on to Elena was proof of her dominance.

"So this girl, Rodari, is your wife?" She said it almost mockingly, but deep in her eyes there was an instant gleam of interest, as if the Contessa had not expected someone so young, so delicately fair, so shy and yet so ready to fight with the self-willed Roman she had married.

"When I heard that my grandson had taken a foreign bride, I thought instantly that she must be a coquette who had inveigled her way into his life. These things happen to rich and successful men, and Rodari is human enough, for all that he resembles a man of bronze." Very slowly that patrician face broke into a smile. "My child, you are not a coquette."

"I should hope not!" Elvi looked indignant. "I was a nurse when I met Rodari. I have, in fact, been a working girl from the age of sixteen." Elvi said it almost defiantly, for this was surely a woman who would be scornful of any bride for her grandson who was not of the Italian aristocracy . . . just as she had been scornful of Sabinetta.

But the years mellow even the most autocratic of people, and the Contessa eyed Elvi with a sort of gimlet respect. "He told me nothing about you! Gave no details. He just sent a brief wire from Rome announcing that he had married a girl who was not Italian or titled. That was a thrust at me, of course. My grandson considers me an unrelenting snob."

"And you thought I was a gold-digger?" Elvi, who dared to do battle with Rodari, found herself suddenly unafraid of this elderly woman who was so frail on her legs that Elena had to assist her into a brocaded, throne-like chair, and to bring forward a footrest for the tiny feet in black satin shoes with silver buckles on them. Seated in that chair she seemed as fragile as a figure carved from old and priceless ivory. Her hands upon the arms of the chair were as tiny as her feet, and weighted with the large-stoned rings.

"I have always maintained that any Italian who marries in his middle thirties is either infatuated with the woman, or bored with his friends. You are no fascinating beauty, so infatuation can be ruled out. Rodari is a Fortunato and as boredom does not run in our bones that can also be dismissed." The Contessa made a seeking movement with her hands, as if this encounter with Rodari's bride had so disarmed her that she was at a loss for words. "Perhaps he married you out of fondness, eh? Perhaps the Roman lion needed a gentle hand upon his tawny hide. My child, how brave and English of you to dare the Fortunato pride!"

"I suppose it was," smiled Elvi, and near her side she felt the stirring of the Roman lion, as if he wished to say impatiently that nothing of the sort had brought about his marriage to a shy English nurse. He had wanted revenge, on Camilla, and on this self-willed old lady who had driven his mother to despair, and inadvertently to her death. Rodari was indeed a Fortunato. Fierce in love, jealous of the family honour, and none too ready to forgive an injury.

"Elena," the Contessa glanced at her granddaughter, imperious, and yet with a look on her face that betrayed a deep, demanding, and dependant affection. "We must have coffee. Please to order some."

"Right away, *la nonna*." Elena smiled at Elvi. "Please take a chair, *cara*. And you also, Dari. You look so large and brooding standing there!"

"I have to be away quite soon," he said. "I am catching

178

a plane for Sicily and will be meeting Lanciani at the airport in Rome."

"That man!" Elena made a face. "He reminds me of a racketeer, with those black sideburns, and those sharp eyes that strip every woman he looks at. Why do you associate with him? He isn't your kind of person."

"Why do you get involved in so much social work?" her brother drawled. "Perhaps at heart we are more compassionate than we appear to be."

"That man cannot possibly need help?" Elena looked incredulous. "The people at the social centre are people in need of aid and comfort. They are worth some trouble and concern, but Nick Lanciani strikes me as an arrogant devil devoted to making money and seducing women. I wonder how many starry-eyed, film-struck girls have found themselves in trouble after being interviewed by that vain Napoleon of the cinema?"

"What a tirade!" Rodari broke into a laugh. "Ring for the coffee while I still have time to drink a cup."

"He is a Napoleon, and I will fetch the coffee myself. Have you time to spare for a pastry?"

"Cherry and cream?" He was grinning as he lounged against a figured column, a hand in a pocket of his narrow slacks. That brooding look of a few minutes ago had vanished, and it was as if the charm of this house, and being in the company of his family, brought memories of youthful escapades, and youthful fancies, such as cherries and cream. Elvi remembered how they had bought cherries in Rome and scattered the stones among the Roman ruins.

For him this Sabine villa could not hold the more tragic elements of the *isola*. Its ghosts and its secrets would not be so personal to him. In any case he would not be staying here. Each tick of the Venetian clock in its golden scrolling brought nearer the moment when he would say goodbye.

Elvi braced herself against the moment of goodbye ... her love for her Roman lion had claws, but still it would hurt to see him drive away from her. She looked at him, lounging there against the column, dark against the creamy stone, but his eyes as they flicked her face sent no message of affection, no promise of a swift return. Would he stay all the time in Sicily, or would his desire to see Camilla take him to her before the night of the ball and the unmasking of the face that was lovely as a camellia?

Elena carried in the coffee and cakes, and it seemed to Elvi as if this last hour with Rodari flashed by on wings ... the wings of some fateful god who planned to keep them apart.

Her heart took a plunge when he glanced at the clock and bent to give his grandmother the ritual kiss on the cheek that was like creased velvet. One of her ringed hands gripped his shoulder and she murmured something in Italian which was inaudible to Elvi, yet which she felt sure was a reference to herself. She went taut and seemed not to breathe when Rodari straightened to his great height and looked at her, a blaze of some indefinable emotion in his eyes ... then he lowered his lashes and the fire of that look was under control.

"I must be off," he said curtly. "*Arrivederci,* Elena. The cherry tarts were as delicious as I remember them. Elvi, come to the car and wish me goodbye."

Imperiously he led her from the house and down the steps to the Lancia, its black bodywork agleam in the somnolent sunshine. Elvi could feel the sun on her skin, yet she felt cold as she offered her cheek to Rodari's farewell kiss. Like a child she was submissive to him, but she heard the impatient catch of his breath as he took her chin in his fingers and turned her lips to meet his own. His kiss held a bruise and she suffered it. Something his grandmother had said had made him wild. She had been unexpectedly approving of his English bride, and had whispered perhaps that when he returned from Sicily they would give some parties for the bride and introduce her to friends of the family. When that happened there would be no easy escape for him from the bonds of matrimony he had forged so recklessly. In Italy the sacraments were still sacred; he had said so himself.

His fingers touched the scarlet scarf at her throat, slid to her shoulder and pressed the fine bones. "It would seem that *la nonna* has fallen a victim to your wide eyes. She has mellowed with the years, so I can leave you here at Corvina without having my sleep disturbed tonight on a balcony in Sicily, where the nights are too hot for sleeping indoors."

"I don't want you to be disturbed about me, Rodari." His touch was sending a chain of little arrows to her heart. "I am sure you have things of far more importance on your mind."

"Spoken like a dutiful wife." He studied her face for a long moment, then he said deliberately: "*La nonna* is right, you are not a fascinating beauty . . ."

"I never shall be," she broke in, and those tiny arrows were piercing her. "You must forgive me if I don't remind you of a southern flower."

She broke free of him and escaped to the top of the steps, and his eyes were fixed upon her as she stood there in her white dress. He seemed to hesitate, as if right now was the moment when he should admit his love for the woman Elvi could visualise so clearly. They might never meet, yet Elvi would always know her rival.

"*Arrivederci.*" He waved his hand carelessly and slid into the car. The door slammed, the engine started up, and a bird flew startled from a nearby laurel tree. His face was turned to her for a brief moment, then he swung the car around and was driving away from her. She listened as it went on its way, leaving silence except for the hidden throb of the cicadas. Her heart throbbed in rhythm with them, and nothing had ever hurt so much, not even the doubts aroused on the island, the knowledge that he had been Camilla's lover. He had gone and she had not wished him a safe journey. At the last moment she had felt too choked to speak, too frightened to betray herself with tears.

She stood a long time alone on the steps, until tinges of the pink sunset began to creep into the sky and the leaves of the trees began to whisper. Why had she not cried out to him: "Don't go, Rodari! I have this feeling that something awful is going to happen!" Why had she held back the words? Only because he would not have listened, or seen the wild appeal in her eyes. Why pretend that she had any sort of a hold over him? Only had he loved her would he have seen the strange, inexplicable terror in her eyes.

Suddenly she heard footsteps and she forced herself to smile as Elena joined her on the steps. "It has been a beautiful day," Elena said, speaking of casual things because she guessed that Elvi was feeling a little sad. "Would you like to stroll around the gardens for a while, *cara*? We have the twin to the Kashmiri tree on the *isola,* and in lots of ways the gardens here are similar in detail."

Elvi could not say that to see such familiar things would bring pleasures and pains too acute, too secret for words, so she held on to her smile and agreed with a little nod of her head.

Iron lanterns adorned the balustrade of the garden court, which they entered through a small iron gate. They walked among hedges of myrtle and laurel, into a magnolia garden like a sanctuary, with a lovely old fountain in the centre and a pool lined with tiles as green as a frog's hide. Lily leaves floated on the surface of it, and large golden fish darted about. Elvi knelt on the stone parapet to trail her fingers in the cool water, and the stone urchins of the *fontana* seemed playfully alive in the gathering dusky pink of the waning day. Birds were flying to the trees, noble old cypresses that had witnessed a thousand scenes of love and laughter and tragedy. The flowers on the pool were like Manet water-lilies, delicately shaded and lovely, and she was wafted back in memory to evenings on the *isola,* when hand in hand she and Rodari had strolled through the gardens. She had held her breath in case the dream should end ... now at Corvina it seemed to her that the dream verged on a nightmare.

She glanced up with stricken eyes and found Elena regarding her with concern.

"What is it, *cara*?" She stroked the fair hair that made Elvi seem fragile in the violet light stealing over the gardens. That made her eyes seem mystic, and her white dress ghostly.

"I suppose I'm being foolish, and moody, but, Elena, it must have been unendurable when you lost Flavio. I keep wondering ... did you have a premonition of trouble? Did you feel the creeping shadow?"

"All the time I had fears." Elena sat down on the parapet beside Elvi, and she took her hand that was ringed and chained with rubies. "I used to sit and watch the motor races and each time I was terrified. When the accident finally happened I could not grasp the reality of it. I had lived through it a hundred times, the flames spreading across the track, the horrified cries of the spectators around me, the agony. For weeks, months after Flavio's death I was like a person in a trance. I spoke, seemed to be alive, but I felt nothing. It went on like that for a long time."

"Poor Elena!" Elvi, all shyness forgotten, leaned forward and kissed the other girl's cheek. "I shouldn't ask you to speak about the tragedy."

"I am glad that at last I can speak of it." Elena's dark

183

eyes dwelt on Elvi. "You love Rodari and so you are afraid for him when he flies away from you for a short while. It's perfectly natural, and he told me over the telephone that you had been a little run down and that Geraldo Rossi had been to see you. Did you like the good doctor? I owe him my reason after Flavio died. He was so kind and he shook me physically out of my torpor. It was he who introduced me to my social work. I see him now and again at the centre. He is one of the few saints I know."

Elvi smiled, recalling that Doctor Rossi had struck her as a man very much in love with the young widow, and one day that love would surely clamour to be heard. It would make its inevitable demands, and then Elena, who had been hurt so young by life, might find a haven with the man who was so different in temperament to the husband she had lost. Older, wiser, and dedicated to preserving life. It was only bearable once for a woman to love a devil.

"I think, *cara*, that you have much heart." Elena stroked the wedding ring that glimmered blood-red as the sunset reflected in the gems. "It was good that Dari should find you when he did. There had been rumours about a woman married to another man ... I should hate my brother to be unhappily involved in that way. He's a Fortunato and we feel deeply, and it was such a relief to meet you, to see for myself that you were a nice girl."

"Nice?" Elvi murmured whimsically. "It's difficult to be merely nice when your husband has a yearning for the beauty he found and lost. Surely you know, Elena, that your brother married me on the rebound from Camilla?"

"And I am glad. His marriage to you will make him forget her. Do you think that beauty is everything? When beauty has gone, where is the heart, the kindness, the soul? What is left but a shell. *Cara,* such women are in love with themselves. They have never learned how to give real love to a man."

184

"But do men know that?"

Elvi's gaze drifted across the garden, which had slowly darkened until the tall trees seemed like shadows, and the classical statues as if they might come alive. The nymphs Apollo had chased. The urchins agleam in the waters of the fountain. The sound of vesper bells drifting down from the hills, lonely, heart-touching, in the warm spicy dusk.

Rodari would be on the jet plane by now, seated beside a window, in discussion with Lanciani about the film ... or deep in thought as he gazed from the window and saw the first pale stars in the sky.

Suddenly, there in the garden of the villa, Elvi went as cold as stone. She jumped to her feet. "Let's go indoors! I ... I want to see lights. I want to hear music. Have you a radiogram? Can we play records?"

"My dear, of course."

When they entered the house the lamps were alight and a maid was pulling the curtains across the windows. Yes, shut out the night, Elvi thought. Shut out the stars. Rodari is up there among them, and I am down here. He is looking at them and that blaze of restlessness is in his eyes.

"I will show you where you will be sleeping." Elena looked at her and saw that the grey eyes had a feverishly bright glitter

Elvi awoke suddenly in the very depth of the night and she lay staring into the velvet darkness, listening to the stillness that was broken very softly by the ticking of a clock. It could not have been the ticking which had disturbed her, and slowly she sat up in bed and stretched her ears to the sounds of the night. They became more distinct, and then her pulses raced as among them she heard plainly the sound of footsteps on the balcony outside her room. For a couple of seconds she was too petrified to move, then she forced her hand to find the lamp on her bedside table. Her fingers felt the switch and she pressed it. At once the darkness fled and into focus came the suite of Italian furniture, the *fleur de lotus* wall-paper, the long curtains behind which the french doors of her balcony stood half-open to the night air.

She tautened, a cry rising to her throat as a hand moved the curtains, lean and long-fingered against the brocade, so that in swift flashback Elvi was reminded of another night, another time, when a man had stepped from her balcony into her room.

She stared wide-eyed, speechless, at the tall intruder. The black hair was wind-ruffled, the driving coat was open at the throat, the eyes were agleam like a night-stalking cat's.

"Rodari!"

"I knew your room . . . the outer doors were all locked and barred . . . *la nonna's* orders because of her jewels."

"Rodari . . ." It seemed unbelievable to be looking at him when she had visualised him far away. Was she dreaming? Then he moved and began to approach the fourposter in which she had awoken, as if her every instinct and nerve had responded at once to his nearness. "You must have climbed . . . you might have broken your neck!"

"You have gone white . . . I frightened you."

"I thought you were in Sicily."

"I never went. I was packed, Amilcare had called me a cab, and I had my briefcase in my hand . . . then suddenly I knew I could not go. I kept seeing your eyes . . . they warned me not to go, and by a strange fate I didn't go. If I had . . ."

He stood at the bedside gazing down at her and she saw that his face was curiously shocked, under the healthy tan. Curiously vulnerable, as she had never seen him before.

"I had to get to you before the morning . . . you would have heard of the plane crash on the radio and believed me among the passengers. You see," he sat down on the bed and his dark, living warmth was very close to her. He seemed to be equally aware of her, and her white cheeks grew warm as the dark eyes she would have died for swept over her, from her tousled hair to her lips, tremulous with so many questions. From her throat so slim and bare in the gossamer opening of her nightdress, to her left hand clenched against her heart, pressing the soft skin with the hard, lustrous rubies.

"You see, Elvi, the plane crashed as it was landing on the airfield at Sicily. Some people connected with the film were there to meet Lanciani and myself. They telephoned the studios in Rome, and a secretary there, who knew I had phoned Nick to say I had changed my mind about going on location with him, then got in touch with me."

Rodari fell silent for a moment, and in that silence he reached for Elvi's hand and slipped his own between the rubies and her breast. "There were no survivors. The plane was burned out on the field, and poor old Nick is dead. He was no angel, but he had his gifts. The film industry will be the poorer without him."

"Lanciani?" she breathed, remembering how alive and vital the man had seemed, prowling the flat in Rome, like a restless panther. "How terrible . . . but, Rodari, how much worse if you had been on the plane. My darling . . ." The words failed her. She could only gaze at him and absorb his reality with every particle of her being. She had known that a shadow had lain over that trip. Her eyes had been filled with that shadow, and she thanked heaven that Rodari had seen it, been warned by it, and was here by her side, touching her, needing her, all other women forgotten but her.

"Out by the car, before I left you, your eyes begged me
187

to stay. All the way back to Rome I kept seeing your face and the look in your eyes. Nick called them clairvoyant, and it's strange that he of all people should do so. When I phoned him before the flight, when I told him I had changed my mind about the trip, he laughed. I can hear him yet. 'Can't you drag yourself away from your little English bride?' he asked me. 'Well, I won't call you a romantic fool, Dari. There was a time when Alice, the witch, could keep me from my work.' "

Rodari heaved a sigh and his arm slid hard and warm about Elvi. "Such a pity their marriage could not last, but I had hopes that Nick might marry again ... if only to give his son his name."

Never, for Elvi, had there been such an acute silence. While it lasted she felt her heartbeats actually merging with Rodari's. With impatience he flung off his coat, and then he held her again, as if he needed to feel her young warmth as close to him as she needed his masculine vitality.

"You remember the girl on the *isola*?" He glanced down at her, a look that sank deep into her grey eyes with their widely expanded pupils. "She almost threw herself from the cliffs ... when I caught hold of her she called me Roberto. I imagine for a moment, with the sun in her eyes, she took me for Lanciani. I imagine he fell for her after Alice left him. When we returned to Rome I tackled him about the girl. I guessed from the look of the baby, and from the name of Roberto, that Lanciani was the girl's lover. He said she was well provided for, but I believe in the end his Italian vanity would have had to claim that child. Such a pity, but that is life. *Questa la vita!*"

Elvi, who had believed such a wrong of the man she loved, sank her head against his heart and pressed to him in penance, in love, in overwhelming desire to hear the whole confession. She longed to ask him why he came to her like this, in the middle of the night, when he could so easily have telephoned in the morning to reassure her that he was alive and not among the victims of the plane crash. Why did he hold her like this, so that only her silk garment and his shirt lay between their hearts? Why did he seem so ferociously loving when it was Camilla he loved?

"I'm so glad you're safe," she whispered, using tame words, gambling with his nature that was strong, proud, and self-willed. Hoping against hope that he would be savage with her and so prove to her that he wanted more ... so much more from her than polite words.

"Safe?" He gripped her and the bruising was heavenly. "Glad? I break all speed limits getting here. I climb a rickety lattice at the risk of life and limb, and you tell me you are *glad*. *Per dio*, I thought you would welcome me with a little affection."

"A little?" She drew her face away from him and looked into his eyes, and her heart turned over to see that mysterious blazing in their depths. "Why should I break my heart for you, when you break yours for that – that woman with whom you had that deathless affair in Venice? You took her to the *isola*. And she spent a night with you at the *palazzo*. I ... I even heard you on the telephone, making plans to meet her at the masked ball ..."

She broke off as he began to laugh, purringly in his throat, like a jungle cat. His eyes were stalking every atom of her face, her bare shoulders, her slim figure.

"So you want to know all about Camilla, eh? She was very lovely and fascinating, like a painting on a wall, or a sculpture cast in pale bronze. I never in all my life knew a woman like her. Her beauty was to be looked at, never touched. Her lips were made for teasing, not for kisses. Her body was there to be elegantly clothed. She was like some goddess, but I was not made to worship from the foot of a pedestal. Yes, she came one night to the apartment. Her fiancé was home from America and pressing for their marriage. She had decided that she wanted to marry me. She would give up his fortune to marry me, but by that time I had grown weary of her vanity. Of pleas not to touch her hair, it had just been coiffured. Of pleas not to kiss her because it smudged her make-up. Of little innuendoes that a woman be treated like a flower.

"Yes!" He said it savagely "She not only looked like a camellia, she behaved like one. The hothouse variety that needs ice to preserve it!"

He and Elvi stared at each other in the lamplight, then with an inarticulate murmur he buried his face in the side of her neck. "At first, *carina,* you were for me an angry sort of gesture against women with their cold, haughty, ungiving pride in themselves. Then I began to love you, to want you with every spark of my Latin fire, but I was uncertain of you. You seemed at times afraid of my desire..."

"Call it love," she pleaded. "Please call it love."

He stared down at her, cradled so close in his arms. "But did I not say it with my body? Every time? Elvi, you must know ... or don't you yet know that actions speak louder than words? Darling little fool, sometimes I wanted to eat you, like a peach!"

"Rodari!"

"Yes," he mocked, "that is my name, and you are mine. *Mia adorata*, tonight, tomorrow, and each day that comes, bringing the nights when I can hold you near to me." He laughed, deep in his throat. "What a shock for the maid in the morning, when she brings your cup of coffee and finds a man beside you. Tell me something, what is all this about a masked ball?"

"I heard you ... you were talking on the telephone, being nostalgic about Venice. I assumed you were talking to Camilla. You said you would see her at the charity ball, and you would know her no matter how elaborate her mask."

"I see." Glinting devils danced in his eyes, and he traced with a fingertip the little line of worry between Elvi's eyebrows. "Did you never hear of tape-recorders, my foolish child? They are machines used by writers to record their thoughts and ideas. I am, you know, writing a sequel to my script. It gives me a better idea of what the dialogue will sound like spoken by the actors."

"Oh ..." Comprehension dawned in her eyes like a pearly light. "I see! You were dictating."

"Yes, and I shall be dictating to you if we have any more of this nonsense about Camilla. Would I want to embrace that statue when I can embrace young living warmth and heart and compassion?" A smile of deep tenderness came into his eyes. "Come, my Sabine, let me kiss you all the way to heaven."

She smiled as she surrendered to him. Tomorrow they would be sad for Nick, and for the girl who had borne his child, but tonight she belonged solely to her Roman, who had come to her through the dark to be consoled.

Her fingers buried themselves in his black hair. "Sabine ..." he whispered, as the lamp went out.